Praise for *Can You Hear Me?*

'Poignantly touches on problems of friendships, families and coming-of-age in a small community in northern Italy. There is much beauty and sadness in this slim novel.' *Times*

'The novel is carried by both the brilliance of its setting and by a scattering of emotional truths . . . It is refreshing to read a novel of crime and darkness that eschews straightforward domestic noir, and Varvello was brave to write about the trauma that haunts her.' *Guardian*

'Move over Ferrante, there's a new Elena in town . . . The novel is something akin to noir, but the emphasis is on the psychological.' *Independent*

'A thriller, a mystery, a coming-of-age story that utterly gripped me from beginning to end.' Victoria Hislop, *Good Housekeeping*

'A beautiful, stark, poignant account of fear, love and loss.' Emma Flint, author of *Little Deaths*

'Riveting and luminous . . . A gorgeous heart-rending novel.' Bret Anthony Johnston, author of *Remember Me Like This*

'A smart, dark, page-turner that lingers long after the last page.' Kate Mayfield, author of *The Undertaker's Daughter*

'Shines a light on one family's black heart, a place where opposites coexist: tenderness and fear; happiness and pain; unfaltering faith and ugly suspicions. A book to get lost in.' Paolo Giordano, bestselling author of *The Solitude of Prime Numbers*

'A book that doesn't shy away from pain – it shines a light on it. And it does so beautifully, page by page.' Alessandro Baricco, bestselling author of *Silk*

'A dark and painful novel, constructed with great wisdom and written with rare restraint.' Nicola Lagioia, author of *Ferocity*

'A world of suspense à la Hitchcock . . . Elena Varvello is a skilled narrator.' Gaia Servadio

'One of the most beautiful, intense and original books I have encountered in my life.' *Huffington Post* Italy

Just A Boy

Elena Varvello

Translated by Alex Valente

TWO
ROADS

First published in Great Britain in 2022 by Two Roads
An Imprint of John Murray Press
An Hachette UK company

1

Copyright © Elena Varvello 2022
English translation © Alex Valente 2022

The right of Elena Varvello to be identified as the Author
of the Work has been asserted by her in accordance with
the Copyright, Designs and Patents Act 1988.

A CIP catalogue record for this title is available from the British Library

Hardback ISBN 978 1 529 36418 7
Trade Paperback ISBN 978 1 529 36419 4
eBook ISBN 978 1 529 36421 7

Typeset in Sabon MT by Hewer Text UK Ltd, Edinburgh
Printed and bound in Great Britain by Clays Ltd, Elcograf S.p.A.

John Murray policy is to use papers that are natural, renewable and
recyclable products and made from wood grown in sustainable forests.
The logging and manufacturing processes are expected to conform
to the environmental regulations of the country of origin.

Two Roads
Carmelite House
50 Victoria Embankment
London EC4Y 0DZ

www.tworoadsbooks.com

To my mother,
who would read for me

Tell all the truth but tell it slant
Emily Dickinson

Just A Boy

2009 (I)

The kids who found it had two spray cans, some loose change, a lighter and cigarettes they'd stolen from their parents.

School was over = summer had begun.

They had sprayed rude words over one of the stable walls and on the shutter of an old restaurant. They'd bought four ice lollies and sucked on them outside the front window of Bar Gioia, watching the cars drive by on the road just outside Cave: a wide straight strip, the tarmac sizzling in the heat.

The only girl in the group kept to one side = a cascade of curly hair and a cherry-red top = under the sun umbrella, sitting on a plastic chair with her knees against her chest. 'Now what do we do?' she asked. 'I'm bored.'

Her father had hit her mother the night before. She had forced herself between them, shouting at him to stop and receiving a kick to her left thigh for her trouble. A bruise under her frayed shorts. None of the three boys knew, not even the one who'd kissed her on the last day of school and she'd since called her boyfriend. She didn't talk about these things.

They threw away their lolly sticks and wandered around Cave, almost empty in the early afternoon, then flung themselves onto the grass next to the playground, sweating through their clothes. They lit cigarettes and the girl took a drag, then started coughing. Her boyfriend kissed her, pushing the tip of his tongue into her mouth. She pulled back, he asked: 'What's wrong?'

They talked about their holiday plans, about music. The girl kept staring at the horizon, the spine of the river, the vertebrae of the hills where they opened up. The tallest boy showed them his phone: a hand-me-down from his brother. He was the only one who had one, and he didn't want the others to touch it.

When they got up, dazed by the sun, their lungs and throats were burning and they had grass stuck to their clothes. As they walked through an alley, they howled at a dog in its backyard; they clung to the gate, pulling faces and sticking out their arms towards it, until a woman stepped out of the house with her hands on her hips. 'Go and bother someone else,' she shouted.

'Fat cow,' they replied, laughing.

They reached the garden centre, the whiteish plastic of the greenhouses.

The girl was walking a few steps ahead, lightly rubbing at her thigh. Her boyfriend took off his sweat-soaked T-shirt, exposing his slender white torso, then cracked it like a whip against his friends' backs and ran away.

At the end of the alley they headed into the woods.

None of them were allowed to go too far on the paths by themselves. A boy had been kidnapped in the woods thirty years before, and the story was still doing the rounds: he'd been found dead, entirely naked, wrists and ankles tied, at the bottom of a ditch in Ponte, only a few miles from Cave. But they were older than he had been – twelve and thirteen – it had all happened so long ago, and they were all together.

Her boyfriend said: 'I saw wildfires, on TV.'

The flames had scalped an entire forest somewhere in the United States. There hadn't been much to it: a small pile of leaves and dry twigs, they said. 'That could be cool,' he said, looking her in the eye, as if trying to prove himself to her. She reached up to him and he draped his arm around her neck, pulled out a lighter and flicked it.

'Can you imagine?' he asked her.

She nodded. She thought about her father, the tightened fists, the tip of the shoe striking her.

She took the lighter from him. 'Yeah, it would be cool,' she replied.

They joined the others, and the shadows swallowed them up.

The light over the treetops looked like melted butter. Sun stains on the gibbous forest floor. No other sound than their footsteps on the path.

They made it to a grassy clearing with an old trailer eaten up by rust. They shook their cans and sprayed paint over a fallen log. Phone boy moved away to wee, then came back and said there was something over there: the glint of metal, a square shape. He pointed, and they went to take a look.

The woods were thicker in that direction. After leaving the clearing, they had to fight their way through thorny bushes, branches as strong as cables scratching their legs.

They began to whisper among themselves about the kidnapped boy in the ditch, looking around anxiously.

'What if someone's here? What do we do?' said one of the boys.

'Let's start with you shutting up,' said the girl.

The shack appeared after a small dip filled with dry leaves. It looked like it was leaning against a tree. It was made of plywood and bits of furniture, its walls half rotten and wrapped in ivy, and the metal sheet roof sagged to the right. The door was almost entirely pulled off one of the hinges.

They stopped at the edge of the dip, waiting. When they realised there was no one there, they found courage again, led by the girl's boyfriend. They all peered inside, into the dense shade that looked like darkness: a disgusting, sickeningly sweet smell. Insects buzzed all around.

'Eww,' they all exclaimed.

They started punching the roof, trying to lift it, then the three boys walked around the outside of the shack. The girl pulled the door back on its one remaining hinge, slowly opening it, held her breath and stepped inside. She could hear the clinking of the metal balls inside the boys' spray cans, the long spurts of paint.

Breathing open-mouthed, she flicked the lighter on, saw an animal and jumped. Her thumb slipped off the button and the shadows returned, slits of pale light cutting into the suffocating space, before she sparked the flame again.

It was a fox, lying on a light blue mat, the white streak of its ribcage shining through strips of flesh and bloodied fur. Its spongy insides were a fistful of flies, and its eyes dark marbles over which the flame seemed to be sliding.

'Come in here!' she called out, but the others were busy laughing.

She shook her hand to shoo the flies away, but they buzzed and filled the space between the haphazardly connected walls before gravitating back to the fox. She moved one step closer to the animal, hesitant, looking around. Dusty objects. A plate. The stub of a candle. A framed photo, face down on the ground. Inside a mug placed on a log, she noticed a toothbrush, some cutlery and a screwdriver.

She pushed her long curly hair over one shoulder and took the screwdriver from the mug. Sitting back on her heels, she reached with the tool's tip towards the fox's neck, and touched it.

'Go away,' she said. She wanted the flies to leave it alone. There was something that looked like a cloth between the corpse and the mat: the blood was dry, the material crunched like frozen snow. 'Come on,' she almost whispered. 'You can do it, get up.' As if the fox, who had come here to die, still could.

Metal rattling. Another spurt of paint.

She squinted at the wound. Her thumb was burning, so she took it off the button again and the flame vanished. She felt a movement in that moment, as if a hand was reaching towards her to touch her, and she leapt towards the door. The daylight outside was a green haze; she could hear her boyfriend calling her, then nothing, not even the buzz of the flies. She turned her head and looked all around: no one. And yet she was sure she wasn't alone. The hand rested on her neck and sharp shoulder blades, grazed her thigh, the greenish bruise, then it brushed against her hair and disappeared. She wasn't afraid, she told herself. No.

She realised she was about to start crying, so she forced herself to step out and take a deep breath.

She was still holding the screwdriver. She hid it in her pocket, covering it with her T-shirt, then joined the others.

'What were you doing?'

'Nothing.'

'Did you find something?'

'No.'

Her boyfriend kicked the wall of the shack and the entire structure shook. 'Careful,' she said. Red and black paint among the ivy leaves. WE WERE HERE. A stylised penis and their three names, only hers missing. 'Let's try and burn this dump,' he said. The shack was falling to pieces – no one would care, would they?

She sniffed. 'You don't mean it,' she said.

'Yeah I do. Bet.'

'No you don't.' Everything felt so stupid now. Her father's face contorted with rage. That entire afternoon. The spray paint. The long narrow valley in the summer heat. A forest on fire.

'It's someone's place,' she added.

'Who cares. Do you see anyone around here?'

The girl stamped her foot. She could still feel that hand, its gentle pressure. 'I don't want to,' she said.

'God, you're boring,' he replied.

He asked for his lighter back and lit his last cigarette. He didn't kiss her, didn't take her hand, but instead started walking with the other boys towards the dip and the grassy clearing, blowing out smoke rings. They became smaller as they moved away, three little shapes, and she stayed behind, staring at the shack.

'It's someone's place,' she said again. It felt important.

She took the screwdriver out of her pocket, put it down in front of the unhinged door that guarded the darkness inside, and reluctantly followed the others.

Fall

The previous week, Sara had woken abruptly with a searing pain running from her stomach right up to her jaw. She sat up, pushing the sheets aside, hooking a finger inside the collar of her pyjamas.

'What's wrong?' her husband mumbled. It was still dark outside.

'I can't breathe, Pietro.'

'Wake up.'

'I *am* awake.'

Here it is, she thought: like a neon sign suddenly switching on in her mind. Here we are.

She slid into her slippers and went downstairs, stopping by the phone, almost about to call the girls. But it would take them over an hour to get to Cave, especially with these icy roads, and Amelia needed to look after the children, and also, why would she scare them like this in the middle of the night?

She stepped breathlessly into the kitchen, switched on the light and let herself fall onto a chair. She touched her left arm, moving up to the shoulder. She had thought she knew what was happening; she'd seen it often at work, in the hospital: mostly men, some too young but all equally terrified. Drained, tense faces, lying on the bed, their hearts betraying them.

'It's okay,' she mumbled to herself as she rocked in the chair, her hand pressed to her chest.

With the life she had been given – that her family had been given – it was inevitable that her heart would eventually fall to pieces. Hadn't she been lucky to reach seventy?

And yet, sitting under the kitchen light, a voice inside her asked why. *It's too soon*, it said. *It's not fair*. Sara thought of Pietro. When he got up, he would find her dead body, slumped over the table. She thought again of Angela and Amelia, and her two grandchildren. Of not being able to tell them: *I'm sorry I wasn't there for you*. But despite all this, she told herself one more time: 'It's okay.'

She closed her eyes and gritted her teeth as the pain shifted to her shoulder blades, colder and sharper, sliding lower. She could do nothing but wait, now, until she slipped into death's dark landscape. She peeled her back from the chair and folded forward, but then the pain subsided, a fist suddenly unclenching – and, eventually, dissipating.

Sara moved her fingers and stretched out her arm, looking at her speckled hand. 'Really?' she said.

She remained there for a long time, still alive, between the old fridge and the Formica cupboards, as if she had missed an opportunity. When she was finally able to get up, switch off the light and head back into the hall, confused and aching, a sudden crack sounded from outside. A branch snapping, or maybe a sheet of ice being stepped through. Sara stared at the dark staircase, stopping to listen. Someone's – something's – footsteps in the snow, followed by silence. She held on to the banister, placing her foot on the first stair. Another sound, a slight vibration this time, made her turn around and head for the door. She turned the key in the lock, cracked it open and looked outside. 'Who's there?'

The light under the porch roof was on. She studied the driveway between two mounds of snow, their car, the empty road beyond the closed gate, and the woods. The night air pinched at her face and bare ankles. The sky was overcast; she could smell it.

'Who's there?' she asked again, her still-beating heart now pushing against her ribs, as if trying to escape from her chest, to the outside.

A cat or maybe a marten looking for food, she thought.

Then she saw a shape – only a glimpse of it at first – leaning against the garage's shutter. She went to close the door, call her husband, but the shape, long and slender, came closer to the light. It moved stiffly but calmly, in a way that was almost familiar, then stopped again. Whoever it was, they were wearing a large dark hoodie that partially covered their eyes, tattered trousers and worn-out trainers.

Sara asked: 'Who are you?'

When the figure lowered their hood, their face was shining.

In the days that followed – an entire week, until the very last moment – Sara tried to hold on to what had happened that night: her legs giving out, her incredulity, then the uncontainable joy, like a glass filled to the brim with the finest champagne.

'It's you.'

Her son had brought his index finger to his lips, shaking his head lightly. *Quiet*. It really was him, twenty years later. His hair was much longer than Sara remembered; it looked dirty and tangled. He had looked at her, then he'd shifted his gaze onto the house, onto the closed shutters of what had been his room until the summer of 1989, and he had smiled. Then he'd taken a step back, another, then another, until he'd turned around and disappeared behind the garage.

The memories after that were a little hazier: Sara must have tried to reach him – her slippers were soaked through with melted snow, her feet were almost frozen – then she must have come back inside, collapsing in the hallway, a thud that had woken up her husband. There had been light on the stairs, she was sure of that much, and Pietro's face close to hers: 'Are you okay? Should I call an ambulance?'

'No.' She hadn't been able to say anything else.

'You're freezing. What did you do?'

Only then had Pietro noticed the open door. He'd closed it and come back to help her to her feet. 'Come on, up we get.'

He'd put an arm around her waist and led her up the stairs and down the corridor, their bony frames moving with difficulty, huffing and sighing, until she was back in their still-warm bed. Then he had lain down next to her and turned off the bedside lamp.

'I didn't hear you go downstairs. You could've woken me.'

'I tried.'

'Where were you trying to go? Are you sure you're okay?'

'Yes, I'm sure.'

'You scared me,' he said. 'I'd just like to know what happened.'

Sara didn't reply. She thought of her son's finger against his lips.

Pietro turned around, his eyes on her. 'So now what?'

'Now we sleep,' she said.

His breathing calmed; a jerk of the leg, then he was asleep again. Sara stayed awake, trying to piece things together: her pained heart, a brief memory of her time as a nurse. Angela and Amelia, and Amelia's children. The noises in the garden. Her uncontrollable joy. Her son must have climbed over the fence behind the garage, fleeing in the night through the woods. She saw the radiance of his face in the cold light. Other than his hair, he hadn't changed; it was as if time had never passed for him.

Maybe the pain had been some kind of summons, she found herself thinking – his presence had been what had woken her so suddenly. *Mum, I'm back.* She had taken a good look. He was still so skinny, lost inside a sweatshirt with the hood pulled over his head.

'Sara, it really happened,' Pietro had repeatedly told her, right after. 'He's never coming back.' He'd try to hug her, but she would push him away, screaming: 'That's not true.'

'I'm sure,' she whispered now, and turned onto her side towards the small mound of blankets that enveloped her husband's body, his white hair, his brow furrowed, even in sleep.

She brushed against one of his arms and heard him sigh.

'Sleep,' she whispered softly.

She felt as though the entire world had held its breath for twenty years, and that it had only finally started breathing again that night.

Darkness still enveloped the house, and Cave, the hills, the woods and the entire valley along the river, from Ponte all the way to Rivafredda.

Before dawn, it began to snow.

Rumours had spread quickly in Cave; Sara remembered it all well.

After the two strange robberies – not serious ones though, not yet – there had been the assault, as they'd called it: he had forced his way into the house of family friends, people who knew him. Everyone had agreed it was an awful incident; really, truly terrible.

He had taken advantage of an open window and caught them in their sleep – Gemma, her husband and their daughter. He had even carried a weapon. Sara had given birth to a criminal, that's what the voices said that summer. Someone violent and unpredictable. Full of anger.

Hadn't he always been a little odd, though? Too quiet as a boy. So kind, always smiling, rarely speaking. She hadn't noticed because she had been blind and deaf, a complete idiot. The rumours were like punches, as was the look that Gemma had given her just before saying: 'Go away. I never want to see you again, Sara, not after this. I don't want to see any of you.'

On the night it happened, Angela and Amelia had gone out together for a secondary school reunion – they both lived and studied in Turin by then. They'd chatted and had a few drinks, had a nice time, but who would've imagined the evening would end like it did? Their old classmates had called them up: *He really did that? Your brother? I can't believe it. How are you? Where is he now?*

Eventually, they'd stopped replying. Angela had said: 'They're like flies on shit.' Her mother had shot back: 'Are we supposed to be the shit?'

Angela had turned and stormed out of the house, passing her father on the porch, and walked up the driveway before disappearing down the road. She'd come back half an hour later. 'Don't take it out on me, Mum,' she'd said. 'I didn't do this. *I* did nothing wrong.' Anger had brought out red blotches on her neck and shoulders, as if she'd rubbed herself with a pumice stone. Amelia had appeared behind her. 'Angi, come, let's leave her alone.' They'd gone upstairs.

Later, Sara had tried knocking on her son's door again, after he'd locked himself inside. He refused to respond, so she busied herself in the kitchen, focusing on cleaning all surfaces with a sponge dipped in water and vinegar. The mixture had splashed onto her dress, creating a wide, dark stain.

'Will they turn him in?' she'd asked Pietro. 'Do you think they'll do it?'

'If the same thing had happened to me, I'd have been to the police already.'

'How can you say something like that? He's your son.'

'How can *you* ask something like that?'

In the morning, the snow had covered his tracks.

The fence behind the garage was warped between two bent posts: he must have twisted it to make it easy to climb over, she thought. Or maybe it had already been like that before last night. She moved the posts, tried pulling them out of the ground, but the knot in one of the links cut her and tiny drops of blood appeared on her palm.

She imagined her son running through the woods, in the dark, branches hitting him in the face. Arriving like a thief and immediately fleeing again; then she hated herself for thinking that way. She licked the blood from her palm. 'It's okay,' she murmured, 'you can do whatever you want. It's okay with me. The most important thing is . . .' She covered her mouth, crying and smiling. She stood for a while, looking at the woods; in the February sky, a coin-sized patch of pale blue shone above the trees, behind heavy clouds. 'Where are you hiding?' She pushed the fencing lower, to make it easier to climb over. 'All I want is to be able to hug you again.'

The patch of blue quickly vanished: shadows fell among the trees and she shuddered. She heard the door open, Pietro's footsteps on the porch, his cough. She waited for him to call her and go back inside. After a while she followed him into the house, removed her boots in the hall and brushed off the sleeves of her grey coat.

'Where were you?' he asked from the kitchen. 'I've been looking for you.'

'I'm here.'

'Were you crying?'

'No.'

He studied her face. 'Are you going to take that off?' he said, gesturing to her coat.

Sara shook her shoulders, then shrugged it off.

She did nothing but wait all day, her heart intermittently jolting like a chained-up dog trying to jerk itself free. She wanted to free herself too and run into the woods, looking for her owner. She told herself multiple times that at that very moment – or maybe in a minute, or in two minutes – her son would reappear.

The air became sharper in the early afternoon: it tasted of metal; of clean, shiny surfaces.

'It's cold, come inside,' said Pietro.

She was sitting on the porch, staring at the road. 'I'm fine. I want to stay here.' He looked at his hands, the dry, rough skin on their backs, and rubbed them on his jeans. He wanted to ask her something, Sara could see, but he just licked his lips and said: 'We need to do some shopping. I'll head out.'

After he left, she headed upstairs, walked down the corridor and stepped into her son's bedroom – untouched in twenty years. She opened the wardrobe, grabbed an armful of jumpers still hanging there and inhaled deeply, then she fluffed up the pillow and pulled the sheets straight, smoothing out the creases on the bottom one.

She went back behind the garage, studying the point where the fencing was warped, her face flushed as if he had already come back and was waiting for her. She blinked fiercely in the bright light.

The sky was lower, layer upon layer of greyish clouds.

'Please,' she whispered, almost smelling the air.

She returned to the house to lie down. She must have dozed off after her sleepless night, because she saw him floating, still a boy, in the clear river water. She heard him asking her to count how many seconds he could hold his breath for, then he'd dive below the surface and she'd count for a short while, until the water grew dark as if it had devoured him. *That's enough now, stop it.*

A car came down the driveway. She heard the crunch of snow being stepped on, a car door being slammed, the front door being unlatched. She opened her eyes.

'Sara?' Pietro's voice came up the stairs.

'I'm here,' she said. She massaged her stomach with her hand.

He brought her a glass of water and placed it on the bedside table. 'Were you sleeping?'

'No.' He was standing against the light from the window and she could only see his outline, the fine hair, the strong line of his shoulders despite his age.

'Gemma was strange today,' he continued. 'The shop was empty but when I walked in it sounded like she was arguing with someone. Maybe I'm imagining things.'

'Maybe,' she replied.

'I got some ham, if you want to eat something. And some oranges.'

'Thank you.'

Pietro turned around to look out of the window. 'Things mustn't be going too well for her. That place seems to be falling to pieces more and more by the day. Too many supermarkets. She should close, really, now that she's alone.'

'She'll do what she wants,' Sara replied. Throughout all these years, she had said so often: *I don't want to waste another second talking about Gemma, not any more.* But at that moment it felt cruel. 'She'll do what she can,' she corrected herself. 'Like we all do.'

Pietro nodded. 'What about you? Are you sure you're okay?'

She said nothing.

Another memory, like an air bubble, rose to the surface: her daughters, barely teenagers, were arguing in Angela's bedroom. He had stepped into the room, stopping between them – his older sisters – and looked at them with a smile. 'He just stood there, smiling,' Angela had told them later, 'and we just burst out laughing.' He was such a good boy.

'I'll get dinner ready,' said Pietro.

Sara felt the empty space he left behind. She thought about calling him back, asking him to sit beside her. She would have told him: *Something happened, last night, something beautiful.* But then she turned her head to the sky, blurry behind the window, and thought about Gemma in the summer of '89, before the assault. A strong, fun woman, who would phone her often in the evenings just to ask her how her day had been, and called her 'stella', star: *Oh stella, if I didn't have you . . .* They had spent dozens of holidays together, children and husbands in tow, exchanging magazines, sun cream, small confessions. Her best friend in the whole world.

The last time Sara had seen her son had been in the bathroom, standing in the doorway, in the pink light of a
summer sunset. He had smiled at her, nonchalantly, and
locked himself in.

'Wait,' she'd begged him, banging on the door. Angela
and Amelia had convinced her to come downstairs and
have something to eat.

She'd sat at the table and they had filled her plate:
reheated spaghetti, a pile of red mush.

'He didn't hurt anyone,' she'd said.

'Yes, Mum, okay.'

'I don't know what came over him, but he never even
touched them.'

From the porch they could hear the sweet, patient voice
of Sara's mother: 'He's a good boy, he's always behaved so
well.' She was trying to convince her son-in-law to come
back inside, to talk to his son.

'Don't you start too!' Pietro had replied. 'Do you understand what he did?'

'Come on, please, eat,' Angela had told her, placing a hand on her shoulder.

A sole forkful of spaghetti: that single bite had congealed in her mouth. She had thrown up, soiling her dress.

'Are you happy now?' As if it had been their fault. She had rinsed her mouth over the sink as the girls stared at her, both shocked into silence. Then she'd headed upstairs to get changed. The bathroom door was wide open: her son had gone back to his bedroom. The moon had just risen over the dark hills.

Sara had sat on her bed. Her mother had joined her; she'd taken a clean dress out of the wardrobe and helped her into it, saying: 'Try and get some rest.'

'I don't want to.'

'I'm sure you'll fall asleep soon enough.'

'I can't, Mum.'

'You'll feel better afterwards, trust me.'

If she had tried to sleep, Sara knew, Gemma's eyes would hurt her again. She would see once more that look of disgust, the one she had given Sara after the assault.

'I feel as though they beat me up.'

'I know, my darling. It'll get better, you'll see.'

'It's like they're still hitting me, one punch after another, right to my stomach. That's how I feel.'

'The world isn't that evil, Sara.'

'You're right, it's worse.'

She had been so tired, though, and the early night, her head on the pillow, her mother's fingers stroking her hair – it all conspired against her and she'd slipped into sleep.

She woke at dawn. She hadn't heard him leave his room, go downstairs, and open the door.

Before dinner she sat on the concrete step for a while, between the porch and the driveway, her coat on her shoulders. She was watching the garage shutter. 'Please,' she kept saying. Her son's face had lost intensity, like a battery losing its charge, and so she closed her eyes, going over its details in her mind.

'Can you see me?' she said. 'I'm here.'

The light from inside the house lapped against her coat and grey hair. A snowplough roared in the distance. She tried to stand, but fell back onto the step like an empty sack. She had to haul herself onto one side, pushing her hands into the concrete.

When she sat down for dinner she was still cold. Pietro poured her two ladles of broth, emptied the pot into his bowl, and switched on the TV. They ate in silence, in the flashes of blue light, slurping at their broth and ripping up slices of ham.

She was watching him out of the corner of her eye. 'Can I tell you something?' she said, eventually. She was thinking about the hospital, she added, about when she worked in A&E.

Pietro nodded but kept his eyes on the screen, kept ladling food into his mouth. They weren't used to chatting.

'There were nights when nothing happened. We just waited. We'd fill out forms or chat a little. I always had a thermos of coffee, remember?'

He nodded a second time.

'I'd think about you and the girls, asleep.' In the warmth of the kitchen, she thought of the darkness just beyond the window. An image of the hospital came to her: the three empty rooms, the quiet waiting room, the staffroom from where you could see the river. It was a small hospital. 'Sometimes I'd feel guilty because I wasn't here with you. You had to cook and look after them and everything.'

'I was happy to do it.'

'I know. I loved you for that, too.'

Her husband frowned; he stopped chewing, then started again slowly. 'You were the one who chose to stay home, Sara. No one forced you to.'

She had left work when he was born, and had never regretted it. But sometimes she felt just a small craving for what she'd given up, a hint of sorrow.

'I know. But I wanted to say that when someone did show up, someone who really needed help, I used to think that we were lucky.' It felt wrong, somehow, for a nurse to feel that kind of relief: like a sweet being sucked in secret. 'Lucky, yes. It just came back to me.'

He shot her a look and turned back to the TV. 'That's not what you said at the time.' He rubbed his cheek, blinking quickly through his dry eyelids, then held up a hand, asking her to wait before saying anything more: the forecaster was announcing that a more unsettled weather front was making its way towards them.

Sara imagined her son in a snowstorm, deathly pale and shivering, his lips livid, wandering the woods around Cave, afraid that someone in town might recognise him. Afraid he might bump into Gemma. She imagined him behind the fence, his hood raised, his eyes fixed on the house.

Pietro took an apple from the fruit bowl and began to peel it. 'It's going to really snow,' he said.

The knife's blade glinted in the light.

One warm, bright morning, a young boy had arrived in A&E. Pale, his hair flat over his ears, he sat in silence in the waiting room. As she left the room next to the main desk, Sara had seen a man talking to one of her colleagues, brandishing a pair of sunglasses. He was pointing at something behind him, towards the double glass doors, his voice raised, asking: 'And what am I supposed to do with him?'

'Please, take a seat, just for a minute. We'll call you as soon as possible.'

'I've been sitting for long enough.'

'I don't know what else to tell you, sir.'

The man had started pacing with his arms crossed, in a rectangle of light.

'What's wrong with him?' Sara had asked her colleague, returning to the desk and looking at the child.

'High temperature. Vomiting. The father says they went to the river yesterday. He was in the water for too long.'

She tidied the papers on the desk, aligned their edges, and sighed. 'How's the lumberjack?'

They had been caring for a man who had slashed his calf with an electric saw while cutting a log.

'Almost done,' Sara had replied.

'There's a lot of the day still to go, though. How hot is it outside?'

'I don't even want to think about it.' Cave was a swamp that day. Sara had picked up a pack of fresh sterile gauze from the medicine cupboard and gone back to work.

'Hold that thing further away from you if you want to stay in one piece next time,' she'd said to the man with the injured calf, as the doctor stitched up the wound.

The man had been clenching his jaw, his eyes on the bloody cloths he'd used on the wound, which were now piled on the floor. 'I have no idea how it happened,' he'd said.

No one ever knew, she'd thought, not even the ones who got in a car completely drunk and crashed it somewhere.

The doctor finished the final stitch. 'Let's get you an antibiotic IV. You'll have to come back for the dressing.'

'My wife was with me,' the lumberjack had said as soon as the doctor had left. 'She was really scared.'

'I can imagine,' she'd replied.

'She can't stand it. Blood.'

Sara had found a vein, hooked the IV pack onto the frame, and gone to call the wife. She was in the corridor, leaning against the wall next to a bed; her eyes were puffy and she was sniffling. Sara had patted her shoulder gently. 'You can go and see him now, he's waiting for you,' she'd said. As she turned around, she saw the boy vomit, so she'd walked into the waiting room and helped him stand up. 'Come on, let's get you to the doctor.' He smelled of Vicks VapoRub, of sour milk, of unwashed skin. There was dry mud on the hem of his trousers, oily patches on the faded material of his yellow T-shirt. The man, who had the same facial features, the same dark hair, had stayed a step behind them.

'Sorry,' the boy had said.

'For what?'

'I didn't mean to make a mess.'

'Don't you worry. What's your name?'

'Luca.'

'That's a lovely name. And how old are you?'

'Almost nine.'

'So you're a big boy.'

She'd let him lie down in the newly vacated room at the back. Holding his hand, she'd asked the father some questions: what symptoms did he have, his weight, any allergies.

'He keeps being sick,' he'd said, wiping his hand across his mouth. He looked younger than Sara, who was thirty-one at the time. He'd answered the questions with difficulty, as if he barely knew the boy. 'We're with my sister, in Rivafredda,' he'd added. 'We came here to see her. We don't live here. She was the one to suggest I bring him.'

'Okay, thank you. Let's see what's wrong with him.'

He'd touched his Adam's apple, pointy like a nail, then put his sunglasses back on, turned around and left the room. The boy shot upright, like a dog being yanked by its owner. 'Daddy!' He tilted forward and was sick again.

Sara had dried the pool of sick and thrown the soaked paper towels into the bin.

'Wait here,' she'd said, dabbing his mouth and chin. She'd taken his temperature, asking him about his favourite football team, his best friend, his favourite ice-cream flavour.

His temperature was really high.

His wide, wet eyes had trailed all the way across the room to the open door: he'd looked terrified.

'Don't be scared, there's nothing to be scared about,' Sara had told him.

She'd only had the girls, back then. She and Pietro wanted another child, and they'd been trying for some time. They were hoping for a boy.

Sara got up from the table and stood by the window. She saw nothing outside, only a reflection of the kitchen behind her.

'So it's going to snow again,' she said.

The windowsill was filled with presents from her grand-children: clay candleholders, a parking disc cut out of cardboard (*Happy Birthday Grandad!*), a tiny crêpe-paper Christmas tree. There were photos of Angela and Amelia: in the most recent one they were sitting together, at opposite ends of the settee. Another photograph of all five of them, in black and white, arranged on the grass by height, her son a little to one side of the group. One of him on his own, a skinny boy on a bicycle, eyes squinting against the sun. Sara caressed it with her thumb.

Pietro started coughing. She turned around and saw him double over, hitting his chest with a fist. She went to the sink, filled a glass of water and handed it to him. 'You need to go back to the doctor's.'

He took a sip, shook his head, and started coughing again.

The previous winter he'd had bad pneumonia: he'd been weaker ever since, even if he'd never admit it. Sara waited for the fit to pass.

On TV, a man with a goatee was pointing a gun at another man; they were standing on barren ground that seemed to reach the horizon. When he fired, the other man fell backwards, his arms wide, raising a cloud of reddish dust.

Sara sat down, placing her open palms on the table. 'Are you feeling better?' she asked.

Pietro cleared his throat with a scraping sound, his blue eyes shining in the wrinkled mask of his face, dishevelled by the coughing fit. 'Not dead yet.'

'I can see that.' They really were old, Sara thought. Her heart shrank. 'My mother,' she said. 'Do you remember how she was towards the end?'

'Of course I remember.' Pietro had loved her dearly. She'd called him 'her special son-in-law', despite him being her only one.

'She'd take my hand and ask me: "Who are you?"' Sara continued. 'She'd always talk about him, as if she expected to see him come back at any moment. I'd get angry, tell her to stop. I understand her now.'

Pietro coughed one last time. 'We did what we could, Sara. We went to visit her. We were exhausted, both of us.'

'Holes in her head, that's what she called them. It must have been horrible.'

There had been old people, in A&E, who would try to bite her hand as Sara was treating them; who would swear incomprehensibly, cursing the world, or stare at the ceiling in a catatonic state. Any end but this one, she used to think – she had been so young; she had a husband she adored, two young girls.

'Everything will be better from now on,' she said. 'I can feel it. I want you to know that.'

He pursed his lips, letting himself slump against the back of the chair. 'You almost fainted last night.'

'Because something happened.'

'What happened?'

'I'm not allowed to tell you.'

She saw her son's finger on his lips again. *Have you gone mad?* Pietro would say, anyway. *That's just not possible.*

'It's been twenty years, Sara; you've hardly left the house in twenty years. Like a ghost.'

'That's not true.'

'It is. It's as though you're the only one who lost him. I'm used to it by now, but twenty years, dear God. How can things possibly get better now?'

A ghost. Right. But he had never left her. He had helped her to the bathroom, helped her get into the tub; he had washed her hair, cut her nails. He had fed her, talking softly.

'That's enough,' he'd say gently, when she started strug-
gling and gritting her teeth, when she said, 'It's all your
fault.' Sara remembered when Pietro used to kick the garage
wall, and she remembered when he'd emptied it, filling
black bin bags, and then driven the car to the scrapyard.
And yet sometimes – though not often – they'd held each
other tightly, in the dark, and she'd whispered: 'I need you.'

'I've done what I can,' she told him.

'I haven't noticed,' he said. 'No one has, not even your
daughters.' Then he turned back to stare at the TV: the
man with the goatee, now unarmed, was watching a young
woman undressing in a dimly lit room.

They both fell quiet, until Sara murmured an apology. 'I
really am sorry,' she said. 'Believe me.'

I still need you.

'Is that all you wanted to tell me? Okay.'

She shook her head, but Pietro didn't see.

The woman on the screen looked starved, ugly even.
Sara watched her walk across the room and open a curtain.
The light hit her, and in that moment the young woman
was gorgeous – just like her son, freed of his hood, had
been last night. Then a shack appeared among dry tufts of
grass. Mountains in the distance. The sky perfectly blue.

'I've never seen this film,' said Pietro.

'Neither have I.'

Sara thought of the man who had fallen in the dust,
shot dead, arms wide like he was on a cross.

They'd all had dinner together, before the assault. It had been a nice evening. Angela and Amelia, back home for the summer holidays, were talking about university – a couple of funny stories – when their brother had asked them to please lower their voices.

'Oh sod off,' Angela had said.

'I said please.'

'We're not even shouting.'

'I thought you were,' he'd smiled. 'Sorry.'

Sara had rubbed a hand on his arm. 'Aren't you warm with that sweatshirt on? Why don't you take it off?'

'I'm okay, Mum.' He'd smiled again, then got up and carried his plate to the sink. He'd paused at the kitchen door. 'I'm going to bed, 'night.' The small fan was buzzing by the fridge. The mosquito coil was lit. His footsteps were light on the stairs.

'What's up with him?' Angela had asked.

'He's probably just tired.'

They had slipped, lowering their voices, into what had been happening in Cave recently: someone had been breaking into empty houses in the middle of the day. A broken window. The items stolen were bizarre, though: a toothbrush, a framed photo, a screwdriver. In one instance, a bathtub had been filled to the brim with water.

'Mum, what did Gemma say exactly?' Amelia had asked her.

'Don't make me say it again. You know – I've already told you. It's just gossip.'

'I just want to understand it better.'

'Well, she says that some guy thinks he saw your brother in front of one of the houses, the one behind the shop. That he recognised him and saw him run away. He's the one who started the rumour. That's it. Can you imagine? Gemma and I had a good laugh about it.'

Amelia had nodded, slightly hesitantly.

'I don't know what's up with him these days,' Pietro had said. 'But something's definitely not right.'

'People only talk because they have a tongue in their mouth,' had been Sara's reply.

'Not always.' Pietro hadn't shaved that morning, and his face looked almost dusty.

'Oh please. They don't even know which house it was supposed to be – Gemma told me as much.'

'Well, he's being strange,' Pietro had insisted, implying: stranger than usual.

The summer evening, still and hot, had rested upon Sara's shoulders.

'I think it was just some kids,' Angela had cut in. 'Someone trying to have a laugh, play a prank. It is kind of funny.' She had shifted her chair, looking at her sister. 'Come on, it's late, we need to go.'

They had taken their father's car.

Sara had gone up to her room. Lying on the bed in her nightgown, she had thought about her husband's words. *He's being strange.* Her son's smiles, his silences, those sweatshirts in the middle of summer. The image of him last week, sitting on the riverbank in front of the small island.

Then she'd fallen asleep.

It was still dark when the phone had woken her up again. She'd heard Pietro heading down to answer it, and the disbelief in his voice as he'd asked: 'What?'

There was a moment of silence after an advert for mois-
turiser. Then the film resumed: the man and the young
woman, newly gorgeous, were now walking along an
empty road. 'I did it for you,' he was saying; she was taking
his face in her hands and kissing him.

Sara picked up her glass of water. 'All I wanted was to
be able to hug him again.'

'We all wanted that,' Pietro said, without looking away
from the screen, as if savouring the taste of that kiss.

The water in the glass looked murky. Sara drank it, then
wiped her mouth. 'I was horrible towards you. I realise
that now. It wasn't your fault.'

A confused dialogue in blueish light filled the silence.

'Please say something.'

He switched off the TV. The only sounds now were the
buzz of the fridge and the ticking of the clock.

'We should have left. For the girls' sake, at least.' He put
down the remote, moved his chair as he stood up, and

looked down at her: his white eyebrows furrowed. The faded blue light of the TV grew darker. 'As far as I'm concerned, this conversation is over.'

Sara shuddered, almost as if a cold wind had thrown the window open, carrying snow into the house. 'I wish you could see inside my head,' she said.

'You sound like your mother.'

'I mean it, though.'

Pietro slammed the back of the chair, making it crash against the edge of the table. He started coughing again; he went to spit into the sink, then rinsed it out. His twig-like legs disappeared within his jeans.

'If you don't mind, I'm going to bed now,' he said.

'Now?'

'Yes.'

'Okay, if you're sure. I'm not tired.'

The one thing she did not want to do – ever again – was close her eyes. She imagined lying down next to Pietro, taking his hand and eventually whispering, *He's back. I know it's hard to believe. We should call the girls.* Then she thought: tomorrow.

It seemed to her that he was staring at the tap. 'What's wrong?' she asked him.

'We all do terrible things,' he said. 'Even if we don't mean to.'

'You haven't done anything terrible.'

'You don't know that.'

He turned to face her. He shoved his hands into his pockets, walked to the door, and when he was caught between light and darkness, he stopped. 'No one is inside anyone else's head, Sara.'

When the doctor had appeared at the door, the boy's eyes darted round to stare at him. Sara had taken his hand. 'Don't be scared,' she'd said again.

'This is a stethoscope,' the doctor had said as he removed it from around his neck to show the boy. Then he'd moved behind him, telling him to take a deep breath with his mouth. Sara looked at his naked back, arched forward; his sharp shoulder blades, his pointed vertebrae. 'Hold your breath. Now blow. Cough. Yes, good, now again.' The boy's gaze had flicked from the metal sink, to the cart's surface, to the oxygen tank.

'What did you do?' Sara had asked. 'Here, where I'm touching you.' He'd had a purple bruise on the lower part of his back, fading into a yellow halo.

'I fell down.'

'How did you fall?'

'Off my bike.'

Sara had studied his small neck and his skinny arms,

and had noticed another, smaller bruise inside his left elbow. A third bruise just above his right wrist, as if he'd been grabbed and dragged along.

'Good,' the doctor had said as the boy wriggled back into his T-shirt. 'Everything looks good. Let's take some blood, okay? Don't worry, you won't feel a thing.'

The boy had frowned and flinched before the needle even touched him. They had taken his blood, given him something to lower his temperature, and hooked him up to an IV.

'This is saline solution,' Sara had said, pointing at the pack hooked onto the thin pole. 'It's like drinking a nice glass of water.'

'I can't drink. I'm sick when I drink.'

'Not with this one, you'll see.'

'Now we just wait for the results,' the doctor had said, and left the room.

Sara had taken advantage of his absence. 'Let me take a better look,' she'd said. Those bruises on his back, his wrist and his arm were definitely strange for a fall. She'd asked him where his mother was, and he'd tried to get up. 'No, no, stay there. You need to try and move as little as possible.' She'd restrained him, gently, for a while. The boy had said something that Sara couldn't make out.

'What did you say?'

'Daddy.'

'Do you want me to call your daddy in here?'

That must have been it, as his eyelids had started fluttering rapidly.

'Okay,' Sara had said, peering out into the corridor. 'I can't see him. Let me go and call him – wait here.' She'd gone to the main desk.

'Do you know where he went?' she'd asked her colleague.

'Who?'

'The boy's father.'

'I think he popped outside.'

'Are you sure?'

'What do you want me to tell you? He's not here.'

The heat on the other side of the glass doors was oppressive, like a warm damp cloth to the face. The tarmac seemed to be melting. She shielded her eyes. Then she'd spotted him leaning against a car door, and she'd walked across the car park. He was smoking: he'd removed the cigarette from his mouth, raised his sunglasses and squinted at her with a vague sense of recognition, as if Sara's face reminded him of someone he couldn't quite place.

'I was looking for you, sir,' she'd said. 'I couldn't find you anywhere.'

He'd gestured towards his cigarette. No questions about the boy – about how he was, or what they were doing to him. He'd merely raised his eyebrows and taken another drag. There were sweat stains on his T-shirt.

'Your son is waiting for you. He's scared.'

He'd shifted his gaze to the smouldering tip of his cigarette. Sara had wondered if he was stupid, or if he didn't care. There was something about him that unsettled her, something in his expression: a frustrating slowness, a touch of arrogance.

She'd taken a couple of steps back towards the A&E entrance, the sunshine piercing the glass, then turned around again. 'Are you coming back in, sir?'

'I don't know,' he'd replied, still focusing on the embers.

'You don't know? Okay, as you wish. If that's how much you care,' she'd said, and her words felt like gulps of fresh water.

The man's eyes had suddenly become smaller and nastier. He'd thrown his cigarette to the ground – Sara had noticed the half-moon teeth marks on the filter – and rubbed the back of his neck. Then he'd slammed his hand against the car door. 'What do you know about what I do or don't care about?'

'I need to go back inside,' she'd said.

'I asked you a question.'

'I need to go back to your son.'

He'd licked his lips. 'The fuck do you know.'

'Great. Well done.'

'You don't know me, you don't give a fuck.' He'd moved closer, the sun behind him, pointing his index finger at her. 'You think I'm a fucking idiot, don't you?'

He could've hit her, she could see it on his face. Slap her
or shove her, force her to the ground. She'd thought: come
on, do it. 'You should be ashamed of yourself.'

'Oh really? And why is that?' A small, stupid smile had
crooked his chin.

'You just should be ashamed, that's all.'

'Tell me why.'

'I have more important things to do with my time.'

Her cheeks blazing, the palms of her hands itching,
she'd turned and was walking quickly back to the hospital
building when the man's voice reached her: 'You fucking
bitch!'

She had pushed open the glass doors and headed back
to the boy's room. 'Your father's outside,' she'd blurted
out.

The boy hadn't seemed to understand.

'Everything's all right,' she'd added, trying to regain
her composure. Then she'd touched his forehead – his
temperature was becoming more normal – and checked
the IV. The bruise on his wrist seemed even bigger now,
stark against the white bedsheets.

'So did your mummy not come here with you?'

He had squeezed his eyes shut.

'Your daddy must have told her. I can call her too, if you
want. Maybe he forgot – it happens.'

'No.'

'I can call her, really, it's not a problem.'

'No.' The dried mud on the hem of his jeans had cracked off when he'd rubbed his legs.

Sara was certain now: it hadn't been a fall. The dad smoking, leaning against the car door. Those small, nasty eyes; that stupid little smirk.

My God, what had he done?

'I know you don't like being here,' she'd told the boy. 'But it's just like going to the mechanic to fix your car when it stops working. Do you like cars?'

The boy had looked at her, resting a hand on his dirty T-shirt: when he'd finally nodded, he seemed to have regained some colour.

Sara had nodded herself in response. 'The really fast ones, right?'

'Yes, the fast ones,' he'd replied.

'Would you like to try driving one?'

The boy had tangled his fingers in the hem of his T-shirt. 'Daddy said he'll teach me, when I can reach the pedals. He's good at fixing them. Sometimes he takes me for a ride.'

'Does your mummy come too?' She'd had this dark feeling that the boy was in danger. He hadn't replied, so Sara had asked: 'Where do you go?'

'He doesn't say. We just go.'

He had pulled his T-shirt up so far now that he'd uncovered his belly, and Sara noticed a line of dirt caked onto his skin. A phone started ringing somewhere; the wheels of a bed squeaked outside the room.

'Does your daddy get angry if you ask him?'

You didn't fall, did you?

But the boy had remained silent.

'You can tell me. It can be our secret.'

'My throat hurts,' he'd said.

Sara had patted the white sheet next to his shoulder, then smoothed it out with the palm of her hand.

The boy had asked her again where his father was.

You fucking bitch.

'It's okay, I'm here,' she'd replied.

No one can see inside anyone else's head, she was thinking now, in the empty kitchen.

She put her glass in the sink, gathered up the tablecloth and stepped outside to shake it out, staring at the darkness of the garage. The clouds were denser and there was a carpet of snow. The icy air burned her face.

As soon as she came back inside, she caught sight of her reflection in the screen where a man had killed another man and had then been kissed by a gorgeous woman, as if the gunshot didn't count. She wondered whether her son had ever been in love, if he had told the person he was in love with what he'd done, if he'd ever talked to them about his family.

'Oh Lord!' she exclaimed to herself. 'Stop this.'

She switched off the lights and went upstairs. There, she opened the door to the room at the end of the corridor, the one where the shutters were always closed, and smelled the dust in the air, the damp odour of the old blanket.

Lying on the duvet in her own room, a few minutes later, she touched her husband's hand: he turned in his sleep, so his back was to her. A blue shirt he had ironed himself — he had taken care of everything these past twenty years, without ever complaining — stood out against the wardrobe door in the impalpable lightness of night.

Sara murmured: 'You mean so much to me.'

It felt like a new language: the words fizzed in her mouth, fresh and good.

She imagined the silent roads, the snowplough's headlights, the skeletons of the trees. She imagined her son appearing from behind the garage wall, calling her softly, and she shut her eyes, listening. Time stopped, suspended for a moment, then folded back on itself, back to the summer of 1989: endless days, muggy weather, slashes of blue in the milky sky.

Everything's okay, Mum.

Her eyes shot open again. Her mouth was dry, and there was no feeling in her arm.

She went back downstairs without making any noise, sat down on the settee and covered her legs with a plaid throw. She could just make out the shape of the half-dead pine tree on one side of the driveway. She suddenly remembered the oppressive atmosphere at the back of Gemma's shop, two days after the assault, her friend's exhausted face and the pile of boxes she had held on to as she said,

'Get out of here, Sara.' She thought of how she'd fled after that. And how, when a few months later Pietro had decided to go back – 'I can't keep hiding,' he told her – Sara had replied: 'You'll be going alone.'

She shoved her arms under the throw and pulled it up to her chin as the night quietly pressed against the windows.

She thought of the empty land between Gemma's house and the woods: a sea of tall grass that her son had waded through. Of the open living-room window, of him climbing through it.

She saw the river again, what they used to call 'the beach' before it became a tip, strewn with rusty bed frames and filthy mattresses, broken furniture, bags of clothes. After the second theft, she had found him one late afternoon sitting with his knees pressed up against his chest by the water, his Walkman headphones – a present from Amelia – clamped to his ears.

She had sat down next to him and turned off the music. 'This was a nice place, once,' she'd said. 'We used to come here all the time, remember? And you used to swim like a fish.'

'It still looks beautiful to me, Mum.'

'Look at the state it's in.'

'Yeah, I see it. I'm not blind, you know.'

He had woken up early that morning, said something about meeting a friend. 'I'll be back for lunch,' he'd said, but he never did show up. Sara had taken the car and headed out to find him. *I could feel you were here.* Her beautiful boy, not even eighteen yet.

'Where did your friend go?'

'I wanted to be alone for a while.'

'You've walked such a long way. And in this heat, too!' She'd squeezed his elbow, and he'd asked her if she hated him.

'What are you talking about?'

'Dad hates me. I see how he looks at me these days.'

'Don't be silly.'

The water had been crystal clear in the golden light, the reeds abundant on the small island.

'That man said he saw me . . .'

'That wasn't you, I know that. And so does your father.'

'Are you sure?'

'Yes, of course.'

'Okay.' He had nodded, pensively. 'Why would I have taken that stuff anyway?'

Upstairs, Pietro coughed in his sleep. Each cough was a syllable, a clear 'no' to every question.

Sara slept very little all week. She ate very little too, as always, but she cooked and looked after the washing, telling Pietro: 'I'll take care of this from now on.' She talked to her grandchildren on the phone, then her daughters.

She thought Angela sounded drunk: she squealed and giggled, taking drags of her cigarette.

'How are you?' Sara asked.

'I'm great! How are you, Mum? Everything all right?'

'I just wanted to hear from you. I'd like you to come and visit; I haven't seen you in so long.'

'Last time you didn't even want to get out of bed.' Angela burst out laughing again, as if she'd just said the funniest thing. 'Anyway, the car's broken down, so I can't go anywhere for a while.'

'What happened?'

'I don't think I want to talk about it right now.'

'Nothing too serious, I hope?'

'Depends on what you mean, I suppose.'

'At least promise me that you'll come over as soon as you can.'

A pause: a sip from a glass or a bottle. Another drag. 'Okay. So you're all right?'

'My heart's been playing up a bit,' Sara said.

'What do you mean?'

'Oh, just an age thing.'

What she didn't say – what she couldn't say – was that she had news about her brother.

It started snowing again, flakes so light they looked like dandelion seeds. It lasted for a very short while: a thin white veil, then the sky cleared again. No blizzard. Sara took it as a good sign.

One windy evening she let herself rest on the settee; her chest felt like thick soup, and her chin hurt. There was a horrible taste in her mouth.

'Are you not coming to bed?' Pietro asked.

She cleared her throat. 'I'm just going to rest here for a little bit.'

He was standing in the living-room doorway, silhouetted against the light of the hall.

'Do you want me to switch the lamp on?'

'No, leave it off, thank you.'

The half-dead pine tree vibrated in the dark; one of its branches had broken off after Christmas, collapsing under the weight of the snow. Pietro had dragged it to the fence, stopping to cough, then hoisted it up and thrown it into the woods.

She could hear the wind rushing, out there, like a river in flood. She thought it was strong enough to shake the house – shake it until it crumbled into ruins.

Just before dawn, everything went still.

With great difficulty, Sara got up and put on her heavy coat, slipped on her boots, wrapped her scarf around her neck, then picked up her car keys and her wallet. She left the mobile phone that Amelia had bought her under a cushion – she never really used it anyway. She closed the front door behind her, got into the car and waited for the engine to warm up.

Pietro was still sleeping.

*　　*　　*

She drove carefully on the frozen tarmac: just an old woman, driving a car in the dark.

What am I doing? she asked herself at every turn.

The woods were black beyond the headlights.

She reached the end of the valley – the bright neon sign belonging to the massive DIY shop with its empty car park, and the petrol station. She turned towards town, drove along the river, crossed the square and the bridge, stopping next to the gym. She sat in silence for a long time, staring at the shop's shutter. She wriggled down in her seat when a shape appeared on the pavement, wrapped up in a light winter jacket: Gemma. She saw her bend down, raise the shutter, step inside and switch on the light.

A bolt of pain shot through her shoulder and down her left arm.

'It was terrifying,' Gemma had told her in the back of the shop, her face swollen and pale. Sara had tried to hug her, but she'd moved away. 'I will never forget it.'

'I'm sorry.'

'You're *sorry*? That's it? You know what I think? I think there's something wrong with you, too. Like mother, like son.'

Sara had immediately thought she was right. It's probably true, she told herself. But then, when he'd disappeared, Gemma's silence – no phone call, not even a note, – had filled her with rage, like an ocean swell building inside her, year after year. But what was left of it now? It had dried up, suddenly, before scattering like dust in the night wind.

Before her dementia, her mother would say: *The world isn't that evil, Sara. There's always a chance.* Sara could almost hear her, sitting next to her. So she removed the key from the ignition, picked up her wallet, stepped out of the car and onto the pavement.

She scraped her boots on the concrete, as if trying to clean them, in the echo of the light coming from inside the shop.

As the bell above the door jingled, Gemma mumbled, 'Good morning.' Then she turned to look at her, frowned and said nothing more.

'Hello,' murmured Sara.

Her scarf was wound around her neck like a noose: the rope was long enough, she felt, to exit the shop and cross the bridge, until it faded out of sight in the chalky morning light. Sara shifted her gaze to the shelves, stood in front of them and picked up a packet of biscuits, pretending to read the ingredients.

At that moment she realised that Carlo, Gemma's husband, would not be appearing from the back of the shop. She wouldn't be hearing his voice from the deli counter. He had died in his sleep, last spring. Sara had felt sad about it, but refused to attend the funeral.

'I don't care,' she'd told Pietro.

'Are you serious?'

'We lost a son and she didn't care, did she? Neither of them did.'

'Why do you always think you know everything?' It was as if her despair had turned into arrogance.

Still holding the packet of biscuits, she glanced over at Gemma, who hadn't moved. Her hair was thin and very short, and she had bags under her eyes, the skin folded over like sagging collars.

Sara moved forward a little, still holding the biscuits. Everything felt so much more claustrophobic – an old, small-town corner shop, its shelves surprisingly empty – and yet, at the same time, fathomless.

She picked up a bag of sliced bread, which she placed on top of the biscuits, then pretended to look for something else. As she was pulling down a box of spaghetti, her eyes glazed over and the things she was holding toppled onto the floor. Sara stepped back and said she was sorry, wiping her hands on her coat. As she was about to flee for the second time in twenty years, she looked up to see Gemma directly in front of her, fuzzy, her head tilted to one side.

'I'm sorry,' she said again. 'I didn't mean to do that.'

'Of course not,' Gemma said, leaning forward to pick up the fallen items.

There was a layer of dirty sawdust in front of the door, and a plastic wreath on the wall left over from Christmas. 'Tanti Auguri', it said.

'Wait, let me do that,' said Sara.

'Leave it,' Gemma snapped. She was wearing faded brown twill trousers, a green jumper and a pair of fingerless gloves. Her scalp shone like new skin after a bad burn.

Sara looked out at February's rising light, the iron sky.

Gemma shook her head and felt the packet of biscuits, the box of spaghetti. 'They're broken,' she sighed.

'I'll pay for them,' Sara said, feeling the noose tighten a little more.

Gemma raised her eyebrows: they were the colour of ash. 'Yes, obviously.'

'I made a mess. But I want to pay for it.'

'You've said that already.'

When the robberies had started, all those years ago, they had talked about them just as many others in Cave had, about the rumours going around town, which had reached Gemma. 'You want to know what I just heard? You'll never believe this . . .' They'd laughed about it. 'I basically saw him being born – I know he'd never do something like that,' Gemma had said.

Those words had lingered, echoing, in Sara's mind for a long time, like a dead animal in the middle of the road that dozens of cars drove past every day.

The empty display next to the till was another thing that Sara noticed. When he was smaller, her son had stolen a couple of caramel bars, hiding them in his pocket.

'You know you shouldn't do that. Promise me you'll never do it again.'

It *had* never happened again, as far as she knew, until that dreadful summer, when Gemma and Carlo and their daughter, Silvia, were sleeping peacefully with the living-room window wide open.

'Get dressed, we need to go out. Right now,' Pietro had told her, walking past her as he'd hung up the phone. She remembered the car journey that had passed without them exchanging a single word, then the house with all its lights on, mother and daughter sitting on the settee, Silvia's face pressed into Gemma's chest.

'How are you?' Sara had asked her.

Gemma had simply stared at a spot in front of her: it looked as if someone had reshaped her features, pulling too hard in some places, pressing violently against others. Her leg jigged anxiously. Behind the settee, the cupboard where she kept the good china was open, all its drawers hanging out haphazardly. Loose papers were strewn across the floor.

'Wait,' Sara had said. 'Let me just go into the other room for a second.'

Carlo had been in the kitchen, wearing a vest and pyjama bottoms, his hair sticking straight up. He'd given them a jumbled account of what had happened. 'I can't believe it,' he kept saying.

'What did he steal?' Pietro had asked.

'I don't give a toss about that. They're terrified! Did you not see them? How do I deal with this? Go on, you tell me.'

'Please,' Sara had begged him. 'Let us go and find him now.'

'Why?'

'Just give us a chance to talk to him first.'

She'd gone back to the living room and, kneeling by the settee, made the same appeal to Gemma. 'Please,' she'd begged, squeezing her knee. Gemma had jerked her leg away: 'Don't touch me.'

Back in the car, on the way home, Sara had burst into tears. 'It can't be true, Pietro.'

'But it is.'

At the end of the driveway, at dawn, they'd stayed in the car for some time. The front door had remained wide open, the light still on under the porch roof and the entrance still in the dark. A trainer lay on its side on the concrete step.

The girls had come outside, up to the car and opened the doors. 'What on earth is going on? He came home ten minutes ago but he hasn't said anything.'

'Where is he?' Sara had asked.

He was lying on his bed in the dark, the other trainer still on his left foot, pressed against the sheet. Pietro had switched the light on, grabbed him by the wrist and forced him to his feet. Then he'd slapped him.

'What, you're a thief now? A criminal?'

'No, Dad.'

'No? What are you then?'

Pietro had dragged him around and he made no protest until Sara had shouted: 'Stop that!' She hadn't really known which of them she was talking to.

'Where's the stuff you took?' his father had asked.

'I didn't take anything.'

'Stop fucking lying!'

'I'm telling the truth.'

The things were on the floor, under the bed. Pietro had gathered them and held them out in front of him: 'So what's all this supposed to be?' Then he'd headed out to return them.

'Why?' she'd asked him.

Her son had smiled at her. 'Could you step outside, Mum?'

Pietro had returned to the house a short while later; he'd bitten his upper lip to the point of bleeding. He'd sat down on the porch without even turning to look at her, as Sara told him: 'He's locked himself in his room.'

'Good.'

'No, it's not good. We need to talk to him.'

'I'm not talking to him. They wouldn't let me in, Sara.'

'What do you mean?'

'They made me stay outside. Gemma didn't want to see me.'

'But what are they going to do now?'

'What would you do?'

Sara had tried calling them, but they'd hung up whenever they heard her voice. Despite everything, they'd reopened the shop two days later, and she and Gemma had talked for a couple of minutes in the stifling space at the back of the shop.

'He didn't run away – that must mean something, musn't it?'

'It would've been better if he had.'

'I'm sure he regrets what he did.'

Then her son had disappeared – there was no other way of phrasing it – and she had broken down: little pieces of her scattered everywhere. That was when she'd started dreaming of a small, dark garden, a shadow crossing it and climbing over a windowsill, her shouting *Stop* and *Come back!* But the shadow in her dreams was only partly her son, only partly related to what he had done.

That shadow – she felt now – was also her own.

Gemma took the broken items into the back, then returned to the main part of the shop. She stared at the floor, her pink scalp showing through the thin tufts of hair.

'I'm sorry,' Sara said again. 'I don't even know why I picked them up.'

She wondered if Gemma still slept in the bedroom she had shared with her husband, or whether she'd moved into Silvia's, which was smaller and had once been papered with posters of singers. Silvia lived in Canada now, or the United States. Did she still wake up in the middle of the night and see a figure in the dark with a hood over its head?

'So you don't need anything else?'

'I don't think so, no. I'm sorry.'

'Oh, God, please stop saying that, it's really irritating. What do you need, then? Do you even know?'

Sara loosened her scarf and undid the top button of her coat. 'I can only imagine what I must look like to you.'

Gemma didn't answer for a few seconds, then she said, 'Old', as if that were the kindest of all the possible answers that had come to mind. 'I must look old to you too.'

'Not really.'

'Is Pietro unwell? Is that why you came?'

Sara shook her head. 'I wanted to offer my condolences,' she said. There was another long silence, and she heard their breathing mix together as her heart began to beat faster. 'Even if I'm too late.'

'You are.' Gemma headed behind the deli counter, sprayed some cleaner onto a sponge and started vigorously rubbing the surface around the weighing scales. 'I think about it often,' she said. 'You might as well know that straight off. There's no point trying to avoid the subject.'

'I know.'

'It still haunts me.'

One of the neon lights started flickering: they both turned around.

'It was Carlo,' Gemma added. 'That night, I'd already picked up the phone. Carabinieri, police, I can't remember who I wanted to call, but he told me to stop, then he called you. He seemed upset for your son; I just hated him. And when you came in here, whining . . .' She dragged the sponge along the chrome side of the meat slicer. 'You didn't know what you were saying.'

Sara nodded, sucking on her lips.

'I haven't changed my mind,' Gemma added, scratching her nose with one of the gloves.

Suddenly, Sara was hit by a thought: it was okay. If she'd been in Gemma's place, if she'd been the one to open her eyes and see, in the darkness of her own room, her best friend's son holding a screwdriver, she would have hated that boy too. And she would have gone on hating him in her memory.

'You're right,' she said. 'I understand.'

'But you never told me that,' Gemma said. 'It sounded like it was only a misjudged prank to you, nothing more.'

'I was only hoping to try and fix things.'

'Sometimes you can't.'

Sara opened the collar of her coat and rubbed her shoulder. Her boy on the riverbank, that late afternoon long ago: they had watched the sparkling water, the small island. *I had nothing to do with it, Mum.* He had seemed sincere. And now he had come back, after all these years.

She must have paled, suddenly, because Gemma asked: 'What's wrong? Are you okay?'

'I don't know how to explain it to you,' she replied. 'I feel relieved.' She looked for something to grab onto, grasping at the air as if she were slipping. She heard her name, barely a whisper – Sara? *Sara?* – something falling to the floor from the shelf next to her, someone's foot-steps, hands grabbing her arms, feeling the coat's material, finding their way under her armpits, touching her back. Had she banged her head?

She found herself sitting on the stool behind the till, her open coat hanging off her shoulders. Gemma's face was a few inches from hers, her breath warm and a little sour. She was moving her lips: it took Sara some time to realise she was asking her what had happened.

'Sara? Can you hear me?'

Gemma's eyes darted like fish underwater and for a second she looked young again.

Later, in the car, Sara would remember the rest of the story: the boy's father, whom she had thought of suddenly

– just a distant glare, at the beginning, as the memory took shape.

She had found him in the corridor again. His arms were crossed, and he looked like someone had told him off since they'd spoken in the car park. He'd looked up at her, and in his eyes, Sara had seen a flash of ice.

'Here,' she'd said to him, holding out the boy's paperwork.

'What's this?'

'Blood count, the results of his physical exam. It all looks good. His temperature has gone down now, but he's still a little nauseous.'

'So we can go?' he'd asked. He smelled of sweat and smoke and warm soil.

'I imagine so.' She would've loved to slam him against the wall. *What did you do to him?* The bruises; the story about the fall; the strange car rides. The mother's absence . . . 'He needs to rest,' she'd added.

The boy had kept asking for his father, but that didn't mean much. He'd still looked incredibly scared. Sara had imagined them sitting in the car: the boy, still, silent, the man's hands gripping the steering wheel.

'This way,' she'd barked at him, turning towards the room.

'Really?'

'I'm sorry?'

'Everything is actually all right?'

'Oh, *now* you want to talk to a doctor? Now you care?'

He'd blinked rapidly, then chuckled, shaking his head. Stepping into the room, leaving his smell in her nostrils, he'd approached his son: 'How are you feeling?'

'Daddy, where were you?'

'I was waiting for you. You're feeling better now, huh?'

'Why didn't you wait here?'

He'd shaken his shoulders, as if shrugging something off. 'You know I can't, I'm sorry. I couldn't do it.'

Just outside the door, Sara had watched them. The boy had hugged his father's hips, resting a cheek against the man's chest. 'They put a needle in me, but I didn't feel it.'

'That's good.'

'I wasn't scared. Like you told me. Just a little bit.'

'Because you're brave, Mummy always said so. Remember? She would say so now, too.' The man wiped his eyes with the palms of his hands, a surprising gesture coming from him. Then he'd helped his son off the bed. 'Let's go home,' he'd said.

They had left together, arms intertwined and clinging to one another, as if they were the only people left in the world. As Sara watched, their outlines had faded in the fierce light beyond the glass door.

The car park scene had remained stubbornly lodged in Sara's memory, becoming more troublesome and more cumbersome as time passed. She had hated him, that arrogant, stupid, violent man. He'd been capable, she just knew it, of twisting his son's arm, striking his back with his fist. But instead, he had been right: what did Sara know, really? She had tried to push the boy's hug and the father's tears into a dark, inaccessible corner, but who had been the arrogant one, really, back then?

Why do you always think you know everything?

As Sara drove carefully home, a feeling of lightness would begin to rise inside her. 'You're a bitch,' she would say to herself, allowing herself a small smile at last.

'What just happened?' Gemma asked, still bent over her, touching her forehead.

Sara put her hand over Gemma's, held it and squeezed it. 'I haven't slept. I've been trying to stay awake for the past week.'

Gemma's expression changed, she became cautious, suspicious. 'If you want, I can call . . .' She tried to straighten up.

'Wait,' Sara held her back, squeezing harder. 'Stay here, please. I came for this.'

'This? What's this?'

'Talking to you.' She took a deep breath. Straightened her back and swallowed, then told her what she hadn't yet told her husband and daughters. 'I saw him,' she said. It hadn't been a hallucination: it really had been him. 'You have to believe me – I saw him with my own eyes.'

Gemma tried to get up again, her face contorted in a grimace, and she pulled her hand away. 'What on earth are you talking about?'

'He was the one who gave me the courage to come here.'

'Who are you talking about?'

'Maybe that's why he's come back, to make everything right.' Gemma's face turned red. 'I'm waiting to see him again,' Sara added.

The bell jingled and Gemma's gaze snapped towards the door, then back at her. She walked over and muttered something to the woman who had just come in, who promptly left again. Gemma lingered in the doorway, looking at the low, grey sky, the bridge, the lights along the side of the hill. Then she locked the door, rubbed her arms and came back over to Sara.

'I can take you home, if you don't feel up to it. I can do that much.'

'There's no need, thank you.'

'But you just fell.'

'And you put me back on my feet.'

Gemma opened her mouth, as if to insist.

'I know you don't believe me,' Sara pre-empted her. 'You should be the last person I tell about this. But instead, you were the first.'

Gemma lowered her head, puffed out her chest and exhaled.

'I'm mortified by what he did to you,' Sara said. 'I will never understand why. It's the biggest mystery of my life.'

'Can we not?'

'No. There are no excuses. When he was younger, I thought that whatever might happen to him, whatever mistake he might make, I'd be able to help him. This is what I used to do, once – I'd try to fix things that didn't work. I helped people. Then, when we lost him—'

'I said I don't want to.'

'He hasn't changed, that's what so strange. He looks the same as he did that summer, as if he's still just a boy.'

Gemma brought her hands to her face, pushed her gloved hands into her hair. Then she uncovered her mouth and sighed. 'You haven't told anyone, not even your daughters?'

'No.'

'You should, Sara. They need to know.'

'Maybe I'm losing my mind,' said Sara. She stifled a chuckle, then a small sob. 'Just like my mother. I'm old enough to end up like her.' She removed her coat and let it fall to the floor. She had considered this possibility, of course, but her son's appearance in front of the garage – that hadn't felt like the product of a rotting mind. Oh God, she thought, please, make it be true.

'We're both old enough,' Gemma said, 'for anything to happen. I don't care how I go, not any more.'

'Neither do I.'

They both smiled at the thought.

Sara massaged her shoulder, then she wiped her forehead and decided to get it off her chest: 'I know it's not possible; I know he hasn't come back. I will never see him again. But a part of me still believes it. Because I love him,' she murmured. And despite the unspeakable sadness for what could never change, she felt the noose slip from her neck, because there was someone whom she could tell.

Gemma lowered her hands. 'I have something to tell you, too.' She took a deep breath. 'I came, you know.'

'Where?'

'To your house. When I heard about your son, what he'd done to himself. I never told anyone.'

'I didn't see you.'

'The lights were off. I tried ringing the bell. I just stood there, staring at the garage and telling myself: this is where it happened, this is where he did it. I was so confused. I didn't ring again; maybe I thought I wouldn't know what to say.' She raised her eyes to the ceiling then removed her gloves, slowly, and put them down next to the till. 'I came back, a few months later, but Pietro was outside. I think he was shovelling snow. I couldn't bring myself to stop and talk.'

'There are so many things we should do, and then we never can,' Sara said.

'We should have done them, yes.'

At that moment, Sara felt her old, tired heart leap, filled with gratitude for what Gemma had just said, and she saw her son turn away and head into the woods. 'We still have some time, maybe. Even if I'm a little mad these days.'

Gemma shook her head. 'No, you're not,' and she told her about Carlo, how much she missed him, how often she felt like he was still there with her. 'I can even hear his voice, sometimes.' She talked about Silvia, who lived in Vancouver and only came to visit twice a year. 'I've always wondered how you felt, even if I was angry and confused. I could only imagine.' Her lips were trembling now.

She must have trembled that summer night, too: Sara would think about it just before leaning against the small table in the hallway of her house, a few hours later, pressing a hand against her chest before she fell to the floor one last time. She must have trembled, yes, lying there in shock and watching that menacing shadow in the doorway.

'I'm so sorry,' Gemma said. 'For everything.'

'I'm sorry too.'

Snowflakes – which would soon become a blizzard – glided in the morning air, but neither of them noticed.

'Oh, please, enough, we sound like a broken record,' Gemma said.

'Maybe we are.'

'Two silly old birds,' she added. But she kept repeating herself, *I'm so sorry, stella*, leaning over Sara, stroking her head in her empty shop.

River

Whenever he reopened his eyes, on those first autumn mornings, Pietro always felt that his son was alive: he was asleep in his room, that's all, and he'd see him soon. The world was a warm duvet, and he was safe inside it.

'Love?' he'd whisper, looking for his wife's hand.

She'd snarl at him, or moan, then rip away the duvet. Pietro would drag himself to the bathroom, head downstairs to make coffee, head back to the bedroom to get dressed, kiss her forehead and tell her: 'See you later.' He'd get into the car, start the engine. Then, and only then, when no one could see him, he'd bang his head – or the steering wheel, or the window – with his fists.

Somehow, he'd make his way to Cave. He'd turn left, taking the road following the river, the water flashing in the barely risen sun, the blaze of autumn leaves. Driving calmed him down.

But there were moments, sometimes, before he left for school, when he'd hear Sara sigh.

'What's wrong?' he'd ask.

She would tap her fingers on the mattress. 'Come and sit here for a second.' She smelled of sweat and withered apples. 'I just remembered something from when he was a boy.' His wife would bring these memories back to the surface: she would pick one, distant and luminous, shake it out and hold it up to the light to show him. 'Remember?' she'd say. Then she'd pick another, and another after that. Then all of a sudden she'd stop, and stare at the floor.

'It's as if they've taken all the breath out of me. There's nothing left. But you look the same as before.'

'You know that's not true, love. You know that.'

The morning light was a white stain behind the closed shutters. Pietro wished for nothing more than to stay there forever.

'Never say that to me again,' Sara had screamed, one late October morning. 'Never use that word with me again. *Love.* Not with me. I can't stand it any more.'

That day – a windy Saturday which encouraged you to stay in bed – he crawled over to her, turned on his side and tried to hug her. Sara kicked out, hitting him in the shin; then she grabbed his hand, brought it to her mouth and bit it.

'Have you gone mad?'

'What else can I possibly be?'

He got dressed, took his keys and headed to the car, a halo of teeth marks on the back of his hand. It had rained the previous night and water was dripping from the trees.

He stopped at a petrol station in Ponte, where a young man filled his tank. Then he moved the car to the edge of the car park, the woods behind him, and watched him serve other customers: he had something of his son about him. At one point, the young man gave him a look that clearly meant *The fuck are you looking at?* And Pietro left.

There was a supermarket close by: he parked behind the returned trolleys, pushed one up to the double glass doors. A wall of warm air, then muffled music; he walked from aisle to aisle, filling the trolley with stuff.

'I don't want to eat any more,' Sara kept saying.

'You want to die of starvation?'

'That would be better, yes.'

'Well, that's not going to happen.'

At the till, a surprised female voice said: 'Hello.'

Pietro turned round and saw the young woman in the queue behind him. 'Oh, hello.'

She was wearing an enormous men's coat over a tight pink T-shirt. Her mass of steel-wool hair, which she kept tied up in school, fell untidily over her shoulders.

'This is a coincidence,' she said.

Pietro filled his bags, paid and put his shopping back into the trolley. The young woman put a tin of tomatoes on the conveyor belt, along with beer bottles, crisps, mince . . . She kept her eyes on him – he got the impression that she had been hoping to bump into him.

'Goodbye,' he said. He headed slowly to the exit, stepped out, and froze just outside the doors: a young couple, clutching each other near the cars, were kissing in the wind.

The young woman caught up with him; she pulled her coat tighter under her chin and asked: 'Everything okay?'

'Yes, thank you.'

'Are you sure?'

Pietro nodded.

'Okay. Well, goodbye.'

But then he asked: 'Do you live around here?'

'A couple of miles away. I walked here.' Her face shone; she wasn't wearing any makeup that day. She must've had severe acne a few years earlier, judging by the small pocks over her cheeks and chin. 'It makes me so sad,' she said.

'What does?'

'That winter is basically here.'

Dark clouds were moving in the sky. The couple walked past them, laughing, the doors sliding open for them.

'I'd better go before it starts raining again,' she said. 'See you on Monday!' She headed for the trolley return area, her own tilting to the left, her coat flapping in the wind. She would have to carry all that shopping all the way back: Pietro imagined her, bags in hand, walking against the buffeting wind.

'Excuse me?'

She turned around, brushing her hair out of her eyes.

'I could give you a lift, if you want.'

Her name was Vittoria, she was twenty-one years old, and she was already married.

One September day, at the end of school, she had appeared at the classroom door with a mop and bucket. 'Oh, sorry!' she'd said. 'I can come back later.'

Pietro was still sitting at his desk, in a square of sunlight, register and book still open.

'No, no, I'm sorry,' he replied. He picked up the items, holding them against his chest, but he didn't stand.

'Should I come back later?'

'No, please, come in.'

He wanted to tell her to close the door and leave him alone, please – *I don't want to leave* – because going back to his wife was unbearable. He would find her still in the bedroom, her face pressed into the pillow and her eyes still wet, or flashing with rage.

'I didn't mean to disturb you,' the young woman said. The T-shirt she was wearing that day, under her unbuttoned smock, had a small target painted on it.

'You're only doing your job.'

There was a small pot plant on the marble windowsill next

to the blackboard, languishing in the lunchtime sun. He pointed to it. 'I don't know where that's come from. I've never noticed it before.'

'It's been there since the beginning of term,' she replied.

'We should remember to water it.'

'Okay, I'll take care of it.' Her leg hit the bucket as she stepped forward, and the water splashed onto her smock. 'Crap,' she muttered as she put the bucket down on the floor. Pietro pushed his chair back, started to get up.

'Wait,' she said, leaning the mop against the wall. 'I wanted to tell you something. I've been trying to since the first day of term. I feel so stupid now.'

'Tell me what?'

'The thing that happened. Everyone talked about it.'

'I imagined as much.'

Everyone really had talked about it, he'd been certain of that; as if he carried a bad smell around with him.

Her eyes started darting around the room. 'I just wanted to tell you that I've been thinking about you a lot. Since I heard about it, I mean. People talk a lot of rubbish when these things happen to other people, but I don't care. Life really sucks sometimes,' she added.

It was as if someone had removed a wet cloth from his throat, and Pietro was able to breathe freely again: it lasted a few seconds, enough time for him to nod.

All of his colleagues had offered their condolences at the funeral, shaking his hand: he had just lost a son. But the thefts and the assault, those had clung to him, those were the bad smell. People avoided him at the school. They'd suddenly go quiet if they saw him arrive, leaving shreds of words wafting in the air: how was it possible he hadn't noticed? What kind of father would raise a son like that? Was he even still capable of teaching?

Fuck them all.

'Did I say something wrong?'

He shook his head. 'Not at all. Just a second.' He took a better look at her: the sharp cheekbones, the hair pulled back at her temples, the dark, grainy foundation. She was incredibly skinny – she had a bad relationship with food maybe, one of those eating disorders that have to do with mothers that he'd read about. She didn't look ill though: in fact, she looked pretty strong. There was something tenacious about her, something vaguely stubborn.

She smiled almost imperceptibly. The light landed softly on her chest, on the small target. She lifted up the chairs, flipping them onto the smaller desks. When she finished, she headed to the window. 'It's still hot,' she said. She dabbed her forehead with her left wrist, the white gold wedding ring shining in the sunlight, and stared at the opposite wing of the school, across the empty courtyard. Then she turned towards him: 'You can stay here if you want.'

Even though it's been thirty years, Pietro still remembers that sentence, as vivid as the September sunlight through the large windows and the leaves of the pot plant.

'You don't have to say anything,' she added.

He dropped back into the chair, watching her mop the floor, her ponytail the unusual colour of steel wool and one of her shoelaces undone, as she said goodbye to some-one else – 'See you tomorrow!' – in the depths of the building, one month after his son's death.

She had arrived at the school in spring. As he held out his hand for a shake, Pietro said, 'I hope you'll survive our kids.' It was an old joke, but she shrugged, thinking he was being serious. 'I've seen worse,' she replied, and he told Sara about it later, after dinner.

'She looks like a teenager with too much makeup, already angry at the world. She's a little aloof.'

'Teenagers *are* angry, Pietro. You see them every day, don't you?' Sara was doing the dishes. 'We've just been lucky.'

They could hear their son's footsteps upstairs in his bedroom, almost pacing.

'And what's her name?' Sara asked.

'Vittoria.'

'That's a lovely name.'

'It doesn't suit her, though.'

Sara had rinsed a pot, put it on the drainer to dry and turned off the tap. 'Maybe it does. What do you know?'

'Come here a second,' he said, slapping his knee. He loved her so much. What did he care, back then, about that spider with her makeup-caked face? He didn't.

That day in September, however, he couldn't take his eyes off Vittoria. He watched her place the chairs back on the damp floor, push them under their desks.

'Call me if you need anything,' she said, back at the door with her bucket and mop. 'Really, any time.' Her blue smock disappeared down the corridor.

Pietro put the book into his briefcase, took the register back to the office, walked across the quiet entrance hall and headed outside. He drove aimlessly, the sun shining over the trees and the water, then headed back to Cave. He could still hear Vittoria's voice. At one point he thought he saw her on the wide pavement looking over the river; but no, it wasn't her, just a young woman with the same bony legs, striding along.

Really, any time.

She'd seemed genuine, as if something bad had happened to her – maybe that's what made her aloof? – and this something, whatever it had been, had brought her there, to his classroom door.

He stayed in the car at the top of the driveway, his fingers on the steering wheel. The sun bounced off the white wall and the roof. He tried not to turn and look at the garage.

His daughters appeared in the living-room window – they were still at home, back then; neither of them had felt ready to leave for Turin again. He saw them talking, moving their hands, then Angela suddenly turned around and vanished from the window. Amelia went into the kitchen, and that's where Pietro found her, sitting at the table with her arms crossed.

'What are you doing in here?' he asked her. She must have cleaned: everything was gleaming. He pulled up a chair next to her.

'I thought you were coming home for lunch,' Amelia said. 'I was waiting for you.'

'I had some work to finish.'

'Mum didn't want to come downstairs; she hasn't eaten anything.'

'She will.'

Amelia looked a lot like him: clear blue eyes, thin lips, strong shoulders. A strong woman, in fact; brave. 'I was waiting,' she said again, and sniffed. She was trying not to cry.

'You need to get back to your life,' he told her. She had just been awarded a doctoral post and she had got engaged.

'What do you mean?'

'You have to get back. You can't stay here.'

She looked aghast. She was considering it, of course, she told him, but 'What about you?' she said. 'And Mum?'

'Don't worry about us, we'll manage. How's Angela?'

'She's gone to her room,' Amelia replied. 'She tore up her notes for some exam or other earlier. She wanted to throw them into the toilet but I stopped her just in time. She says it doesn't matter anymore.'

It doesn't, she's right, Pietro thought – just like the table he was sitting at didn't matter, or the house or Cave or the whole valley. It was all an open, bleeding wound.

'And what did you tell her?'

Amelia looked at the ceiling, her lips even tighter.

'Okay, don't worry. I'll talk to her, it's okay.'

'Daddy?'

'Yes?'

She didn't say anything else.

The following day her fiancé came to pick her up. Amelia said goodbye to her mother, in her bedroom, came back downstairs and tightly hugged her sister, who had refused to return to Turin. She kissed Pietro on the cheek; he smelled her hair, then he took her fiancé's much stronger hand in both of his. 'Take care,' he told him. He watched them disappear beyond the gate, his eldest daughter's head on her fiancé's shoulder.

Angela, standing on the porch, was chewing one of her nails. 'Take care of what?' she asked.

Not long afterwards, it started drizzling. A cold mist rose from the valley. They ate dinner in silence, just the two of them – Sara hadn't got out of bed – then Angela went out. He waited up for her, sitting on the settee in the dark as if he was underwater with a stone around his neck. At four in the morning he heard the car coming up the driveway. He saw her sway into the hall, struggle to take off her shoes, her bag slung haphazardly across her body: she must have been drinking.

'You can't drive if you're going to get into this kind of state,' he said.

She snapped round, then switched on the light and put her hands on her hips. 'Oh, fuck off, Dad,' she sneered. 'I'm not like you.'

'Like me how?'

Cold, her eyes said. 'I've never seen you cry. You never talk about him. And you went straight back to work.'

'What should I have done?'

'Stayed with Mum.' She slid a cigarette from the pack she had pulled out of her bag, lit it and blew a mouthful of smoke pointedly in his direction. 'So fuck you,' she said.

'You started smoking?'

'Always did.'

Amelia and her fiancé came to pick her up one October Saturday. Before they all set off, Angela said, 'Wait a second.' She disappeared behind the garage and came back a few minutes later, her face wet with tears.

Later, on his youngest daughter's unmade bed, Pietro found a notebook: Angela's tiny handwriting, the pages filled with her brother's name. The weight of that name – the enormous rock around his neck – pulled him to the floor, his back against the bed and his hands pressed to his mouth.

Vittoria and her husband, a large young man with a shaved head, were renting a run-down farmstead on the outskirts of Ponte. Attached to it was some land dotted with trees, sloping down towards the river, and from the upstairs windows, she told him, she could see patches of water. She hated the valley, but she liked the water. Because she was a Scorpio, she added. 'What sign are you?' she asked.

The dirt road, filled with holes, ran straight through the woods up to a flat area of concrete screed. Upon it stood two pillars of bricks, but no gate or fence, and there was a stable with a caved-in roof on the left side of the court-yard; planks belonging to a bridge had been thrown into the neglected garden. The farmstead's wooden frames were flaking and the plaster was mouldy. Against the outside wall, next to the door, was an old sofa.

What feels like a century later – now – Pietro wonders whether the farmstead still exists, or if it has been demolished.

*   *   *

That Saturday morning, when he first gave her a lift, Vittoria gave him directions up to the pillars. 'Here we are,' she said, frowning as she looked at the house, as if considering how ugly it actually was. 'We were in Rivafredda before, where my husband works. That garage after the Esso petrol station – not sure if you know it?'

Pietro tried to remember if he'd ever been to it.

'It was just too expensive,' she added.

'How long have you been married?' he asked. She was so young.

'Two years.' Vittoria raised her index and middle finger, tiredly waving them in front of her. 'I feel old if I think about it.' She rummaged in the bags at her feet and found what she was looking for – crisps. She opened the packet and offered it to him.

'No, thank you.'

Vittoria grabbed a handful from the bag. 'We had a fight this morning, that's why I walked,' she said. 'He took the car, went to his parents. His *beloved* mummy.'

'And you like it here?' he asked her.

'It stinks of mould, and there are too many trees,' she replied with her mouth full. She wiped her lips with the palm of her hand, and rubbed it on her jeans.

They sat in silence for a while on the muddy road, the sky heavy with rain.

'He's not back yet,' she said. 'He'll be there all day, I bet, complaining about me.'

Her husband usually drove her to the school and sometimes picked her up too: Pietro had seen him, leaning against the bonnet of a burgundy Panda. She would walk quickly across the courtyard and he'd open the car door for her, as if for a child. He seemed like a decent man.

Tongues of wind licked at the leaves of the trees, and a darker shadow fell over the broken roof of the stable. Pietro thought of his son – his lifeless body and purple lips – as he'd pulled him out of the car, in the garage, yelling: *Wake up!*

Come on, please, wake up.

Today is a warm April afternoon. Pietro gets up from the armchair where he's fallen asleep – an eighty-year-old man, who has begrudgingly survived the death of his son and his wife – and heads to the kitchen, his arthritis-deformed hands pressing on his kidneys. There are two slices of apple on the counter next to the sink, surrounded by already withered peel. He listens to the ticking of the clock. He imagines his son, his elbows on the table, it's as if he can hear him.

Who knew you could do such a thing to Mum? You had principles, didn't you, Dad? You never did anything wrong.

You don't know what happened after that.

Of course I do.

You weren't here.

Of course I was. I always have been.

He leans against the sink, as tired as if he's been running or dragging furniture from one room to another. He eats the two slices of apple. The April sun, now that the half-dead pine tree has been taken down, falls freely across the entire floor.

Then he hears Vittoria's voice, next to him in the car.

'I imagine your house is much nicer.' She pulled out a last handful of crisps from the packet. 'Virgos care about their possessions.' Her crunching grew slower and slower, as if she were pondering something, then she added: 'Maybe I should keep my mouth shut for a little bit.'

'Why?'

'To avoid saying anything fucking stupid. With what you're going through.'

'It's true, though,' he told her. 'I did use to care.'

There was almost nothing that Pietro could not fix, keep alive. It was terrible, if you really thought about it. When his son had been very young he would follow Pietro everywhere, especially during the long, light-filled summers, studying his toolbox, the tins of paint and the roller brushes, or the shears.

'I want to do it too,' his son would beg.

'When you're older,' he'd reply.

'You can see it on your face, you know,' she said, now. 'I don't need a fancy degree to read you.'

Pietro had asked her what she meant.

'You keep everything inside.' There was a damp,

soil-like smell in the car: it seemed to come from that giant coat she wore, or maybe her hair. 'As if it were your fault.'

'It probably is.'

Vittoria shook her head. 'No.' She crumpled up the empty crisp packet, shoved it back in the bag. Leaves trembled around the dirt road. 'I believe you think too much, that's the problem. Thinking too much doesn't do any good.' She drew concentric circles in the air. Then she tapped her temple: 'There's a lot of space in here.'

Pietro managed to force the tiniest of smiles.

She told him that sometimes, at night, she'd open the bathroom window just a crack and listen to the river. 'When I can't sleep. I think I can hear it – it's a nice sound. All that water rushing.' She brushed the crumbs off her pink T-shirt. 'You have a mark on your hand,' she said.

'It's nothing.'

Vittoria's hand moved closer to his, still on the steering wheel, landing on the outline of his wife's teeth.

'You can always try,' she said.

'Try what?'

'To empty your head.' She grazed his arm, reaching up to his shoulder; Pietro held his breath. 'Isn't that why you gave me a lift?'

It had already started at school, when Vittoria had said *You can stay here if you want*, but he only realised it at that moment. A powerful current washed over him and he turned around and looked at her lips, her cheekbones, her mass of hair.

'I can't let you come inside,' she said.

'I know.'

'And we can't stay here.'

Pietro moved the car to the side of the road, then Vittoria said, 'Come,' taking him by the hand. They walked across the courtyard. There was a small structure behind the house: a mound of wood, next to a pile of pallets, and a block in which someone – her husband, most likely – had wedged an axe.

Vittoria rested her back against the wall and licked the back of his hand, piercing him with her brown eyes. He leaned down to kiss her, hesitant at first, and she opened her lips, salty and sticky, and all they did for a while was kiss, but then she said: 'Wait.' She slipped off her coat and dumped it over the pallets; raised her T-shirt and bra in the cold wind. 'You like it?' she asked him. Her breasts were as white as baby teeth and her nipples dark. She told him to suck them, then she unbuttoned her trousers and did the same to his. She took him in her hand and whispered in his ear: 'Do you feel it?'

'We shouldn't do this,' Pietro said. There was a smell of soil in his mouth that he could almost taste.

Vittoria's hand was incredibly warm. She batted her eyelashes, the tip of her tongue between her lips. She told him again that no one was home. 'I'm on the pill, don't worry,' she added.

He had the impression that she might have brought others behind the house before – that it might be a habit – while her husband was at work or at his parents', and that thought dissolved all his reservations, erased the dirt road in the middle of the woods and the one leading to Cave, his wife's face, that feeling of the wet cloth shoved down his throat.

'Turn around,' he told her, because as horrible as this was, he was still alive. He slid her jeans down her legs, then her underwear, as if peeling her.

Vittoria moaned, then started panting.

'Quiet,' he said.

When he finished, he rested for a few seconds against her back: her breathing vibrated against his chest.

Then she slipped away. She straightened out her clothes and told him to wait: 'You can't use the bathroom.' She came back with a piece of kitchen paper, her hair undone and a black tracksuit top over her T-shirt. She had a red mark on her cheek, like a graze.

'What did you do, there?'

She shrugged.

'I'd better go home now,' Pietro said.

'Okay.'

'I've never done this before. I want you to know that.'

'I didn't ask.'

Before leaving, still gripping the piece of paper tightly, he caught a glimpse of his reflection in a window speckled with raindrops. He had just turned fifty.

Vittoria walked him to the car and picked up her shopping bags. He started the engine, the driver's door still open.

'I don't know what to say,' he said.

'I'll see you in school,' she said, putting a hand to her cheek. 'Thank you for the ride.'

That was the day that Sara had shouted at him that she no longer wanted him to call her '*love*': he could've gone to the river and drowned himself in it, for all she cared.

When he returned home, she screamed all afternoon. *You slapped him and called him a criminal. It was all your fault.*

Her mother came to visit them in the evening. They sat in the kitchen, talking about Sara, who had fallen asleep.

'You need to give her time, Pietro.' She stroked the hand that Sara had bitten, then she asked him what year it was. 'I keep getting confused, these days.'

'I can drive you home, if you want.'

She touched one of the buttons on her cardigan. 'I still know how to find my way back.'

'I'm not sure I do.'

Once he was alone again, he went outside to kick the garage wall. Vittoria's house was out there, somewhere, down behind one of the hills.

The thuds echoed in the darkness.

'There's nothing nice here except for the river. Scorpios love water, I told you that. It's our element.'

It was early December. It had snowed overnight – just a sprinkle – and the dirt road and fields looked like they'd been covered in ash. After sunset, darkness had enveloped the car like a wet pillowcase. From the spot he'd parked in, on the country road, they couldn't see the river.

'I'm not that nice either,' Vittoria added, pulling a lock of hair down over her eyes.

'Stop that.'

'It's true. Not like it fucking changes anything.' She arched her eyebrows, the tip of her tongue like a lick of flame between her lips, her eyeshadow smudged across her eyelids like a bruise. 'You like it, don't you? When I talk like this? I'm a bad girl – you should spank me.' She shifted in the car seat, turning her torso towards the car door, and slapped her bottom, two quick, light slaps; then she sighed and sat back down again. 'Hello? Are you there?'

Pietro looked back at her for a few of seconds. He switched off the interior light, as if scared that someone might show up; it could happen, it might do.

'Yes, I'm here,' he said.

'I can see that. Wow, thanks.'

She leaned towards him, unfastened his belt buckle, undid his trousers, then leaned in further.

'You don't want to go in the back?'

'Does it make a difference?'

'It doesn't, no,' he said, and he ran his fingers through her hair, grabbed a handful and pulled, pushing the back of his head against the headrest, biting at the cold air, his legs burning. Vittoria's head seemed to be bouncing against his groin.

A few minutes later, as Pietro was cleaning himself up with a tissue, she wiped a hand across her mouth, like a brushstroke. She curled up in the seat, squeezing her knees to her chest and resting her chin on them.

'What's up?' he asked her.

She'd suddenly lost all her brazenness, that lack of modesty that allowed her to give herself openly, riding the waves of remorse and regret with ease.

'Nothing.' There was a pause. 'It's just . . . we're invisible. We can do whatever we want and no one will notice.'

'Better for you this way.'

'For both of us.'

'It doesn't make a difference for me,' he said.

She lowered her gaze to the black carpet. 'You're worse than usual,' she said, plucking something off one of her shoes, but then she chuckled and rubbed her lips against the stretchy fabric of her jeans. 'Are you feeling better now, at least?'

Pietro nodded.

'But nothing really lasts that long, huh?' She picked up one of the loops of her shoelaces with her index finger, as if it had fallen into a puddle. Her mass of hair was hiding her face. 'I shouldn't have said that.'

'You can say whatever you want.'

Pietro turned the key in the ignition, lowered his window and threw out the tissue: it glided over a thin layer of snow. In the distance, the neon sign of the DIY shop shone in the darkness, and headlights on the main road pierced the valley back and forth.

Vittoria untied then re-tied her shoelaces. 'We need to go,' she said. He started the engine and the car slid on the dirt road, like a vein in the middle of the fields, and she massaged the back of his head, jostling in the seat, her nails gently scratching his skin.

'Your hand's cold,' he said.

He would have preferred — he often felt this way, after sex — for her not to move, not to say anything, until she left the car.

'Well, nothing else is,' Vittoria replied, in one of her bursts of brazenness. She added that they should have kept the engine on while they were doing it. 'Or maybe bring a blanket, at least? I almost froze to death last week.' She told him, yet again, about her never-warm bedroom, about a leaky heater and the stove that had stained the entire kitchen wall and a good part of the ceiling with smoke. Pietro pretended to listen, nodding every now and then. He pretended to smile when she smiled.

It wasn't that Vittoria always wanted to talk: there were days when she was nervous and would keep clicking her tongue against the roof of her mouth, or rapping her knuckles against the window, and on those days he'd feel the need to ask her what the matter was.

'What do you care?'

'Could you not just say it?'

'You don't want that.'

She would shake her head and brusquely order him to kiss her – 'stop wasting time' – or she would shove her hand between his legs, then slither onto the back seats and pull down her jeans. But most of the time, she'd be in full flood: she'd complain about her ugly skin and her dry hair, or a fingernail that had broken as she was cleaning a blackboard, or the number of blankets that she and her husband had to pile on the bed to stay warm, and that weighed them down like heavy armour.

Shivering, Vittoria did up her coat. She moved her hands closer to the flow of warm air from the heating vents, turning them as if roasting them over an open fire. She told him about a student she'd caught writing on the walls of one of the bathrooms.

'I pretended not to see him; I did the same at his age.'

'What did you use to write?'

'Who knows. I didn't go to school often enough to remember. Things about boys, maybe. I could write something about you, now.'

'It would shake things up a little, at least.' He briefly told her about the glances from his colleagues in the teachers' room. What he imagined they thought of him.

Vittoria stuck out her tongue in disgust, then murmured: 'Pieces of shit.'

'That's a euphemism all right.'

'What does that mean?'

'Nothing.'

'Sounds like an insult. You nasty euphemism!' She pulled one of his earlobes, giggling.

When he was next to her, Pietro had the impression that part of the life energy that ran through her leaked out of her body, oozing through the inside of the car, penetrating and expanding through his own body. There were things he could ask her to do, after he'd finished pretending to listen to her – things she would do, and he was surprised every time at how quickly she'd fire up, as if she'd done nothing else but wait for him as she mopped the floors or carried papers between classrooms. On good days, she'd mutter: 'Yes, that's good, yes,' or 'Again', with such sweetness, even if she always got dressed so quickly afterwards. Sometimes, while he was still inside her, Pietro could hear Sara's voice travelling through the woods, running along the fields over the cold ground: *Just look at yourself*. So he'd thrust a little harder, take Vittoria's fingers and put them in his mouth, come, and collapse on top of her.

After they'd crossed the bridge, Vittoria said: 'I've never asked you what you do when you go back home to your wife.' She was drawing a damp circle on the fogged-up window, and quickly erased it.

Pietro shook his head. 'I don't want to talk about it. You know that.'

Vittoria pressed her hand against the glass. 'That pot plant,' she said. 'I always remember to water it.'

He kept driving.

They'd meet every Wednesday – because her husband worked until late, she had told him. Pietro came to pick her up, then they'd drive down hidden country roads. He had made clear from the start that he would never talk about his son, or his wife, or his girls. About what had happened that summer.

'Don't ask me anything about it.'

'Sure, okay.'

They'd fuck, bumping against the roof and the doors, and she'd take him in her mouth or in her hands; then, before heading back, they'd just sit, breathing heavily as if they'd just escaped a building on fire. Vittoria would start talking. Sometimes she'd burst out laughing as she told him about this or that piece of gossip, 'Wait, listen to this,' she'd say, with such speed it was as though her teeth were trying to escape her lips.

One day she told him that the fall of the Berlin Wall had reminded her of her eighteenth birthday party in an abandoned house in Rivafredda. A couple of boys she didn't know – stoned or drunk – had tried kicking down one of the walls.

'It's not exactly the same thing,' he said.

'It was fun though. And at least I was there for that one, it wasn't just something I saw on TV.'

The world was sinking, outside the car: the dark clumps of ploughed earth in the fields, the border of the woods, the hazy lights of distant houses.

Vittoria kept glancing at the mirror in the passenger sun visor. 'I should cut this stupid hair. Or maybe dye it red, I don't know.'

'What would that change?'

'Fuck, you're worse than my mother. *What would that change?* You're not listening to me.'

No one at school noticed what was going on: the casual waves of greeting and small talk about the winter greyness of the mornings continued as usual.

He would see her yawn, leaning against the heater in the entrance, in her smock and heavy makeup, as the students filed in in groups. Those were the moments when he thought the two of them should stop. There had been practically nothing about Vittoria that had piqued his interest, before. Even now, there was almost nothing that struck him about her; only that pinched look of bitterness when something seemed to go wrong for her. Maybe the hunger that pushed her towards the back seats, the way in which she offered herself. Pietro felt the need to go back home, lie down next to Sara and ask her for forgiveness. But then there were moments, during a class test, say, when he'd see the pile of pallets again, the axe in the chopping block, Vittoria's white breasts, the red mark on her cheek. As his students' pens scratched over their papers, he could feel her tongue lick the back of his hand like a cat.

Just one more time, he'd tell himself.

On Christmas Eve he dreamt that he'd pushed her to the ground, in a field that stretched to the horizon, pushing her head into the mud and opening her legs. He was wielding a screwdriver – each thrust was one strike – and suddenly they were in front of the farmhouse and his son was there too. Only then did Pietro realise he had hurt her.

'I didn't mean to.'

'I didn't feel anything.'

'Are you sure?'

'It was him, anyway, not you.'

When he woke and opened his eyes, his teeth were chattering.

His daughters, home for the holidays, were already whispering downstairs in the kitchen. Angela started to sob. Pietro smelled smoke, the sound of pots and pans. Amelia said: 'We need to move forward, Angi.'

During that winter, Sara's face became sharper. A white sculpture, with a long, smooth neck, angry tendons, ruthless slits for eyes. It comes back to him now, in his old age, as the April light fades and the shadows reach out across the new grass in the garden.

He thinks back to how his wife lived in their bedroom. She only went out on her own to visit her mother, in the Rivafredda care home, and to take flowers to the graveyard. She always had terrible headaches. One of her teeth split in two, but she refused to see a dentist until it hurt so much that she felt she was losing her mind. She said something was nibbling on her gum. 'It's like having a small animal in my mouth.'

She couldn't stand any physical contact. She forced him to sleep somewhere, anywhere, else. 'We have so *much* space now, don't we?' she spat at him, and for two weeks Pietro moved into Amelia's room, where he would wake up constantly from brief bouts of nervous sleep, thinking of his son's eyes, hidden by his hood during the assault, his heavy body in the unbreathable air of the garage. And then came the thoughts about Vittoria, like lumps of ember covered in ashes, with her too-big coat tucked up against her back and her jeans around her ankles, on all fours.

'I'm coming back in here tonight,' he told his wife one morning, at dawn. 'Whether you like it or not.'

Sara curled up on her side.

'Enough now,' he said. 'We have the girls.'

'I am alone, Pietro.'

Sometimes she seemed to be feeling better. She was in no physical pain, so she'd take a shower and get dressed – but then she'd burn an egg, overcook the pasta. She'd sit with Pietro at the table, and in those moments it was as though he was enveloped in warmth, as if the sun had peeked out from behind the clouds, but it would soon be gone.

One day Sara spat out a mouthful of food onto her plate, then wiped her mouth clean and lifted her gaze to meet his.

'I wonder how you do it, how you're able to,' she said. 'Leave every morning.'

'I go to work. I can't just stop.'

'Go to work. Eat. Breathe.'

'I'm pretty sure you're breathing too.'

She pursed her lips, then pushed the chair away as she stood up. 'If I were braver, I'd stop doing it.'

'Never say that, not even as a joke.'

'I wonder why I haven't done it yet.'

Pietro heard her footsteps going up the stairs, the bedroom door closing. He screamed; a silent scream in the empty kitchen. To love someone and not be able to do anything to stop them from fading. Or to not understand in time – before there was no time – what they needed, what secrets they were hiding.

'Scorpios and Virgos aren't compatible.' Vittoria said she had read this in a magazine, while the hairdresser fixed her hair. 'It's the top pairing on the "No" list.' It was getting dark. She pulled a face; her coat was zipped all the way up to her chin.

'So?'

'So I'm a Scorpio, a water sign.'

'You've said that before, yes.'

'And you're a Virgo, which is an earth sign.' She turned round to look at him. 'What is it that you don't get, exactly?' She had never gone out with a Virgo, she continued. Or only once, just for a few days, when she was fifteen. 'He was a little shit who thought too much of himself, with a tiny dick.'

'We're not *going out*,' Pietro corrected her.

He shooed away the image of her as a teenager lying on the back seats. The ease with which she had led him round the back of the house, that first day, leaning against the wall.

'You can call it what you want.'

They had driven down a dirt road along a fruit orchard, the skeletal trees in the darkness – and stopped where the road opened up a little. There was no light around.

'A little shit,' Vittoria said again. Something crossed her gaze.

'You don't actually believe in that stuff, do you?' he asked. 'Astrology?'

'I should be with a Pisces – that would be the best. I've never had the chance.' She blew onto her hands. 'Holy fuck, it's even colder than usual. Turn the engine on again or come over here, so I can stop talking.' She began to suck on a lock of hair, but he pulled it out of her mouth, lowered the zip of her coat, and shut her mouth.

In early March, he saw Gemma's car approach their house, slowly, and then drive away again.

It was a Sunday morning, early. A tinfoil sky.

He was using a spade to break up a pile of frozen snow in front of the garage shutter. He had stepped out to get some fresh air: that pile of snow, grown larger through the winter, had suddenly looked horrible, something he should erase.

He struck it with the edge of the spade, kicked it with his boots and snapped off some chunks, stepping on them to crush them. A thin nail of sunshine scratched at the clouds so insistently that it broke through. That was when, surrounded by lumps of snow, his hands burning, he saw her drive by. As if she'd meant to stop, but then, seeing him brandishing a spade and stamping something into the ground, had thought better of it. The father of that demented boy.

He told Sara about it when he headed back in to change his clothes.

'That's not possible,' she replied, her head on the pillow, a white sculpture. 'She doesn't want anything to do with the two of us. She can go to hell as far as I'm concerned.'

Pietro kept thinking about it; in his mind, he kept seeing the car slip by, the dark surface of the closed window. A few days later, he parked his car in the small car park next to the gym and crossed the road.

Gemma's eyes looked as if they were vibrating when he appeared in the shop. She took something from the till and headed into the back.

'I don't know what to say,' Carlo told him, but then asked: 'How are you?'

He started dreaming of the assault in more faded, nuanced ways: the shape in the darkness, crouched in Gemma's garden, wasn't his son; or maybe it was, but it had no screwdriver and would leave immediately, heading for the woods.

Sometimes, in his dreams, his son was a child bringing home small trophies: an empty tin, the foil paper from a piece of chewing gum. A stone. A twig.

'I found it on the road.'

Pietro always woke up crying.

Around then, Vittoria started telling him she was thinking of leaving her husband. She made a point of saying that their relationship – 'or whatever you want to call it' – had nothing to do with it.

They had just got dressed again. The sunset light washed out the DIY sign.

'I deserve better,' she said. She pulled down her cardigan and started blurting things out: 'I was only sixteen, when I met him; I'd stopped studying. And living with my parents was crap. He was already working, all the girls were after him.' She told Pietro about a warehouse, just pillars and a roof, lost in the countryside, and how much she loved spending time there, in his car, with the doors open and the radio on. 'He always used to say he loved me. Now he comes home from work and just sits on the settee in front of the TV. He doesn't even move when I start yelling; just stares at me and asks me if I'm done.'

'I always thought he was kind,' Pietro said.

'I told you I want to leave. I have my reasons, okay?'

'Where would you go?'

She looked at him as she touched her cheek, those small craters.

'I'm only twenty-one. I deserve better,' she said again.

Pietro suddenly felt like grabbing and shaking her, shouting in her face that the world was a hellscape; she had no right to complain: she hadn't lost a child. All he said was: 'I'm not the right person to ask for help.'

'I didn't ask you anything.' She started rapping her knuckles against the window as he drove her home, towards Ponte. Before she got out, she asked him: 'I'm not completely worthless, am I?'

Later that evening, Pietro called his daughters. He talked to Amelia for a couple of minutes, asked her about her fiancé. He tried comforting Angela, who had burst into tears: 'I still can't believe it, Daddy.' He could hear her sobs through the miles of cables, and puffs of her cigarette. 'Where's Mum? I want to talk to her.'

'She's already asleep.'

'Daddy?'

'Tell me.'

'I keep thinking about him. I have so many memories.'

Pietro wished for her to be blessed with light and radiant images.

A coughing fit: the old feeling of drowning, his lungs underwater. The sun has set and the sky is a thin, deep blue strip. In the fridge, on the highest shelf, are the remains of the cake his daughters bought him for his eightieth birthday, last week. It's not looking good: the strawberries have blackened and the cream has liquefied.

'It was Mum's favourite. It's already been ten years,' Amelia says, peering out of the window at her children, on their phones in the driveway.

They're about to have lunch together, a small party.

'So, how are you doing, Daddy?' Angela asks him.

They'd like Pietro to sell the house, they said so again today, and for him to move into town.

'You can't stay up here, it's too isolated. What if something happens to you?'

'It would be weird if it didn't, at my age.'

'That's not funny,' says Amelia, turning to look at him.

'Never been a funny guy.'

Angela smiles.

Pietro would have moved, that summer, but Sara couldn't even bear to think about it; it was as if the place had become hallowed ground.

'I miss Mum,' Amelia says. Angela nods.

They both remember her voice on the phone, that final afternoon; her tone light, her words unexpected: *I feel good, at last. I love you – I always have.*

'I'm not alone up here, anyway,' he says. 'I won't rot when my time comes.'

'That's true.' Angela has recently got married, at the age of fifty-two: she's still surprised about this herself, she says. She quit smoking and drinking a long time ago. 'Speaking of, Daddy, isn't she late?'

'She'll be here soon.'

Pietro has never told them Gemma's story, what she told him after Sara's death, during a sudden, unexpected visit – Gemma coming into the house wearing a winter coat reaching her feet, her boots crusted with snow. 'Still the same in here,' she remarked, looking around. Then she sat down on the settee. 'She fell ill while she was in the shop, but I didn't realise it was so serious. I was worried you might not believe her, Pietro; that's what I thought it was about.'

'What should I have believed?'

'She didn't tell you?'

'No. What is it?'

Sara's vision. Their son in front of the garage shutter.

Gemma squeezed his wrist. She muttered: 'I think it really happened, you know. She somehow actually saw him. I'm a mother too.' Before getting back in the car, she added: 'Please call me, if you want some company.'

Another coughing fit, in front of the fridge. Pietro covers the remains of the cake with some tinfoil: it's not time to throw it away yet.

'Come on, Daddy, you're eighty years old,' Angela said on his birthday. 'We need to celebrate.'

'I'm happy to see all of you again. That's more than enough.'

His sons-in-law's voices, from the living room: politics and work. His grandchildren's voices on their phones. Then a car, a door slamming and Gemma's voice: 'Stop fiddling with your phones, kids, and come and say hello.' For a second, mistaken for Sara's.

'Here she is,' he says, getting up.

In spring, Vittoria fell ill for two weeks.

One late afternoon, in light drizzle, Pietro turned onto the dirt road, driving slowly, then pulled over and noticed that the lights in the farmstead were off. The Panda was in front of the entrance, parked on the concrete screed, next to a clothes horse draped with washing. She had never talked about her husband again, about leaving him, nor had he asked her how things were going.

Among the wet washing, he noticed Vittoria's oversized coat.

Sitting in the car, the engine still running and the windscreen wipers swishing, he felt something similar to pangs of hunger – a dull yearning for her to join him, for her to open the door and get inside, saying, 'Let's go.' He almost heard her voice: 'We're invisible, no one ever notices us.' And it was true, it really was – then he felt his son's presence move next to him. He thought, as if he could ask him: tell me where I went wrong. He held his head in his hands.

The only sound was the drumming of rain, nothing else.

In the days that followed, he tried to focus on his work. He went through and marked piles of class tests. He tested unprepared students, feeling truly sorry for their pursed lips, angry spots and braces, the way in which they'd sway in front of the blackboard.

'Let's try again next time,' he told his quietest student, who was torturing one of his fingernails as he stared at the equation he had been asked to solve. Pietro smiled and watched him return to his desk. Then he turned his head, glancing at the pot plant which had survived the long winter.

Vittoria came back to work in early May. She had lost weight – her eyes looked bigger under her pasty eyelids, her cheekbones sharper – and her skin was rough terrain.

At first they didn't speak, in the noisy entrance hall, simply stared down at their hands and feet. Then he asked her how she was feeling.

'Better.' She touched an elastic band around her wrist. 'I saw you, from the window. You were in the car. It was raining.'

'I came over, yes.'

'Wait for me at the junction. Tomorrow afternoon.'

And so he drove to pick her up. They passed the closed cotton mill in Ponte, the brick wall lined with bottle shards, and kept going through the woods. Pietro turned onto a path, stopped the car at a small grassy spot. He was sweating, his armpits damp beneath his cotton shirt. He turned to look at her and she did the same, eyes wide, and they started kissing, tenderly. Then they pulled apart and caught their breath.

'We've never been here,' Vittoria said.

'I wanted a change.'

'I'm still a little tired.' One of Sara's gloves was in the glove compartment: Vittoria took it out, measured it against her own hand. 'I fucked up,' she said.

She told him how, one night, she'd left the house in just her underwear and trainers, had walked down part of the dirt road.

'Where were you planning on going, dressed like that?'

'I don't know. It was so cold. I headed back and curled up under the structure at the back. That's how I got ill – fucking bronchitis. They stuffed me with antibiotics.' She let out a little laugh, as if she found everything so stupid. 'When I was much younger, I tried to leave home. So it must be something that's just there, inside me.'

'Running away?'

'No, fucking up. My husband brought me back to bed that night, when he noticed I wasn't there. I saw him switch on the lights and he started calling me.' She said he had run outside, scooped her up in his arms. 'Maybe I'm crazy. I don't think you care, anyway; you're a broken thing, maybe we both are. Someone needs to fix us first. Find the pieces scattered around and try putting them back together. I don't seem to be able to.'

She put Sara's glove back.

'Vittoria is mad, mad, mad,' she hummed. 'And you're a Virgo, so precise.' She took his hand and kissed one of his knuckles.

'Please stop,' Pietro said. 'Don't say you're mad. It's not true.'

But she kept repeating it, moving his hand as if keeping time, then she guided it under her T-shirt, against her warm skin. She placed it between her breasts, where her heart was beating fast inside the cage that held it.

One June evening, after a solitary dinner, Pietro went to sit on the porch. He unbuttoned his shirt, removed his shoes and socks and placed his feet on the cool ground, looking at the unruly grass.

He heard Sara's footsteps in the hall, saw her walk outside and sit down on the step. She was wearing her pyjamas, and her hair was stuck to her neck. She rubbed her arms and looked up at the sky, a dark blue table upon which someone had cast luminous dice.

He kept staring at her: she was in the same exact spot where – so many times – their son had sat. It felt like the rest of the world, beyond that step, had disappeared after his death; it had been plunged into darkness and there was no way, not any more, of crossing that threshold.

Nothing happened, Sara simply sat, rubbing her arms, but as he looked at her he realised he had never even considered leaving her, throwing away what little was left between them. He realised he would never have another life, and he didn't care that she no longer tolerated his presence, or that she blamed him for what had happened.

You were right, he thought, I should've knocked at that door. Forced it open with my shoulder or my feet, if necessary; told him that I didn't understand why he had done it, or what had been going through his mind, but I cared about him and I would have helped him even if I didn't know how.

'I love you,' he said.

Sara didn't hear him: she crossed her arms tightly over her chest, her eyes still gazing up at the sky.

He turned towards the garage and apologised to his son, that shadow walking across a lawn and climbing through a window: *I'm staying here. I'm not leaving.*

He was where he had always been, despite not knowing, not anymore, where that was. People were free to think whatever they wanted about him.

He told Vittoria that they should stop. 'It's not your fault,' he tried to explain. 'You haven't done anything wrong.'

She had removed her sandals and her bare feet were up on the dashboard. She flung a hand out of the window. 'Of course it's not my fault.' Then she closed her fingers into a fist, as if she'd grabbed a handful of air.

'It's just that I can't keep doing this,' he said. He saw her clench and unclench her hand. 'What will you do about your husband?'

'Who knows?'

Pietro thought of the large young man with the shaved head and the muscly arms who sometimes waited for her outside school, and who had found her, one night, half naked under the outdoor shelter, had picked her up in his arms and taken her back to bed. They were both so young.

'You shouldn't throw away what you have,' he told her.

'Fuck, you sound like an old man now.'

Her toenails were painted black: she pointed at them, asked him if he liked them.

'They're interesting,' he said.

She smiled. 'That's good, then.'

'But really, it's not your fault. The opposite, in fact. I should thank you.'

'What for?'

'For what you've done for me.'

Vittoria chewed her lip. 'I did what I wanted when I wanted to.'

'Okay.'

'That's just how I am.'

Pietro studied her face, the fold of her mouth. The sun was shining on one of her shoulders.

'I always meant to ask if your daughters look like you,' Vittoria said.

'Only my eldest.'

She rubbed her finger over a toenail, as if trying to remove the polish. 'What about him? Did he look like you? It's just a question. We're not going to see each other again anyway, or at least not like this. Right?'

'I don't think so, no.'

'If he looked like you, he would've been cute,' she said, then lowered her voice. 'Why don't you tell me what happened?'

'You already know.'

'I didn't mean *that*. I mean what happened after. To you.'

He turned away, towards the trees; he heard Vittoria sigh, pulling her legs off the dashboard and putting her sandals back on.

'When I tried to run away from home, I tried hitch-hiking. I was thirteen,' she started telling him, as if Pietro had asked her. 'A bloke and his wife stopped and I got in. I could see them looking at each other every now and then, then she turned around and started just staring at me. It was weird. Plus, the car reeked of wet dog and rubbish, and there were hairs everywhere. The wife asked me where they could take me. I lied to her: I told her I had missed the bus and that I was going to school. Because school was close. I just wanted to get out of the car, you know? I was starting to get scared, because she was staring at me.'

Pietro turned back to look at her, then he leaned forward, resting his head against the steering wheel. He could see her knees, her thin ankles.

'So we got to my school and there was no one else around; it must have been maybe 9 a.m. I was about to leap out of the car but she grabbed me by the wrist and squeezed hard, so he told her to stop, and she started crying. Not sobbing, just gentle weeping. She told me they had recently lost their only daughter and that I looked just like her. She would love it if I wanted to go and live with them. I could wear her clothes, sleep in her bed, use her things.'

Pietro noticed she was holding her right arm, just above the elbow.

'For a moment I thought I could do it.'

'Really?'

'I asked myself: I wonder what it would be like. I could've become someone else.'

'Then what happened?'

'The man told her to stop it immediately, she let go of my arm and I got out of the car. Then I went home.' She took a long, deep breath. 'Yeah. I think about both of them sometimes. I never saw them again, but I remember them. I think it's important. I remember them well – that's something, right?'

There was a dead leaf in the footwell; Pietro, his forehead still on the steering wheel, brushed it with his foot.

'That morning I woke up abruptly,' he said. 'My son wasn't in his room.'

After the cake, on his birthday, they've cleared the table and are now looking at old family photos. Gemma was the one to suggest it: 'Before I forget what you all used to look like.'

Some of the photos have her and Carlo in them too, relaxed and smiling. Gemma points at one, saying: 'I remember this one,' then slaps a hand on her forehead. 'Gosh, I remember it as if it were yesterday.'

Amelia, standing between her two sons, looks like she's about to cry; one of the boys drapes his arm around her shoulders.

Pietro is looking at the photos, then at Angela and Amelia, his sons-in-law, his grandchildren, and Gemma, with her thin hair, the tender pink of her scalp. Gemma, who came to the house after his wife's death to tell him what Sara thought she had seen. Who came specifically to tell him: 'She was happy, you know? In her mind.' To tell him: 'It's just the two of us left now, you and me.'

Gemma has paused over one faded photo of a paddling pool in the shade of the once-luscious pine tree. Her daughter, a tiny little naked thing, sits with her feet in the water.

'That's Silvia,' she says. 'And that's him.'

Next to the pool is Pietro's son, eight or nine years old, holding the girl's hands.

'I don't think I've ever seen this one,' Angela says, as her sister begins to sob. 'It's a lovely photo.'

Gemma narrows her eyes. 'I wonder who took it,' she says. Then she caresses the girl's face on the faded paper, as small as her little fingernail and filled with joy, and his face, busy holding up her daughter, looking down at the water in a tangle of shadows.

This is what he told Vittoria: the door wide open at the end of the corridor, his son's empty bed, him bolting downstairs and looking everywhere for him and then going outside. The muffled muttering of the engine from the garage.

'As if he was about to leave, that's what I thought,' he said. 'Even if he didn't have his licence yet.'

He told her about the air filled with fumes, about how he had pulled him out of the car, completely naked, how he had knelt next to him, on the floor, throat and eyes on fire, opening his mouth, blowing into it in vain, holding his arms as he told him, over and over again: 'Wake up.'

'Then I heard my wife's voice and I ran back out.'

He had held her in his arms, he said, pushing her onto the grass so she couldn't see. He had held her, and she had struggled, shouting at him to let her go. And when the girls had come out, he'd cried: 'Call an ambulance!'

He could remember the sky turning lighter, he added. The wailing of the sirens. The darkness inside the garage.

'I left him on that floor. Right there, all alone.'

'What else could you have done?'

'I should have stayed with him. Sometimes, during those final months, he used to stare at me as if he wanted to ask me something.' He slammed his forehead against the wheel. 'If only he had asked.'

'Stop it,' she said.

'But no, he never did.' Pietro continued to head-butt the steering wheel: he felt no pain. 'I've never been able to cry, not in front of them. Never. What kind of fucking person am I? You tell me.'

Vittoria lifted his head from the wheel. 'You're crying now,' she said.

'Why didn't I stop him?'

'Because you didn't know.' She stroked his head, as if all their encounters had been like this, this kind of gentle affection, not the fast, hungry sex they'd actually had. 'You need to go home, Pietro.'

He wiped his face, then he cleared his throat and hugged her.

When they turned onto the road to Ponte, Vittoria told him that she wasn't going to say goodbye: she was simply going to get out of the car, run inside, and that would be that. Pietro needed to leave immediately, without dithering or wasting any more time.

'Don't even think about it, okay?'

'I'll try to remember.'

She leaned her head out of the car window and closed her eyes. 'Look at us!' she cried to the world. 'Can you see us now?'

Not even Gemma knows this story – the year of cheating. The way in which that young woman kept him alive, as if Pietro was a pot plant.

I haven't forgotten.

He tried breathing deeply, to calm his cough.

In his mind, he drives along the river, all the way to Ponte, across a couple of junctions and finally onto the dirt road. To Vittoria's house at the end, the two pillars and the peeling frames, the weeds in the courtyard and the woods around it. The small roofed structure at the back.

After that summer, she and her husband moved: Pietro heard someone talking about it in school. He doesn't know where she went.

He imagines Vittoria shivering in the cold, under a pile of blankets, or maybe standing in front of the window while her husband sleeps, trying to listen to the sound of water.

'I see her,' he whispers.

It's dark by the time he gets in the car, puts on his glasses, switches on the headlights, buckles his seatbelt, and starts the engine.

He has spoken to Gemma on the phone: 'Everything's okay, yes, I'll see you tomorrow,' he told her, then hung up and started coughing again. Then he said: 'I'm heading out for just a second, okay?' as if he was expecting a reply: Sara's voice, his children's voices.

He will stop on the long, narrow dirt road; he'll take a quick look and then head back home and to bed. He hasn't done this in thirty years, and he will never do it again.

'I used to come here, once,' he'll say. Nothing else.

What happened to them both? Where have they ended up?

Vittoria, hitch-hiking. The man and woman who had seen her on the side of the road. Sara, sitting in her pyjamas on the concrete step, in the spot where the world had disappeared. And above everything else, him: his boy, that unfamiliar shadow with a hood over his head.

Pietro imagines the lights still on and the open windows. The stable roof has been fixed, the walls re-plastered, the frames painted. There are flowerpots. A new family. Small children, perhaps. Someone will open the door, as if they had seen him, and raise a hand in greeting: 'Hello, can I help you with anything?'

Pietro will raise his in response. He will do so kindly, in the evening air, then shake his head. April, the river in the distance. And everything will be forgiven.

Camps

They set up the tent in the early afternoon, on a grassy field with a stream running through it.

'I don't know if I'll be able to sleep in here,' Angela said.

'Of course you will. Thread the pole into the loop. Good. Now let it slide.' Amelia helped her pull the canvas along the pole and planted a peg into the ground.

'Is this good?' Angela asked. 'I've never done this before.'

'It's great.'

Once they'd finished, they stood next to each other – not close enough to touch, of course – and looked at the tent. The sun beat down amidst clouds of insects, under the beating sun.

'I promise you it's comfy – there are usually four of us,' Amelia said. 'Why don't you try lying inside for a second?'

Angela felt suddenly breathless, as if they'd locked her inside a wardrobe or a dark cupboard – it had happened often enough, when they were girls. Her sister would dare her: 'Let's see if you're brave enough,' knowing full well how much small spaces terrified her sister. She would lock her in the broom cupboard in the corridor – or sometimes in the cellar – and although she tried not to, Angela would end up sobbing as soon as she heard her sister move away. Amelia never really left her alone for long; she would open the door again before Angela could start screaming, the light in the corridor behind her, a smug expression on her face. She would take her hand and they'd go and play, as if it had all been a bad dream. Angela had always had the impression that affection was a reward, a prize to be gained. It was all implied – their silent pact, sealed with clammy hands – that she would never tell their parents. In fact, Amelia hadn't ever truly forced her into the cupboard, or the damp cellar with its dusty little window. It was more of an unspoken question: 'Will you do this for me?' Later, sitting on the carpet in her bedroom, safe and sound, peering at her older sister's face, Angela would be overwhelmed by a feeling of utter gratitude. But where had her mother and father been, in those moments? Her brother?

'You'll be completely fine, you'll see,' Amelia said, pointing at the tent. 'All you really need is a nice, long sleep, trust me. Just step inside.'

Angela shielded her forehead. 'I don't want to right now.'

'Okay, as you wish. I'm so happy you called me, though.'

They headed back to the car, walking through the woods along the shady path, to unpack what was left: the freezer bag, the rucksack with the camping stove inside, a plastic bag filled with food, and two folding chairs.

Amelia passed her the chairs and the freezer bag. 'You got this?'

Angela nodded. There was only one other car nearby, its bonnet pointed towards the valley and a constellation of stickers covering its rear window.

'Okay, let's go.' Amelia closed the boot, put the keys in her pocket and walked ahead of her on the path. 'What a lovely day,' she said. She started humming: '*E lei piangendo sentì mancarsi il cuore*.' She stopped to ask Angela: 'Do you remember this one?'

Angela did not – and she was already panting, even though her load was pretty light.

'That's not possible! We used to sing it all the time when we were little.'

'Maybe that's why, then,' said Angela, and she saw her sister shake her head and laugh abruptly. 'It's true,' she went on. 'I can hardly remember anything from when we were younger. I must take after Nonna; I'm becoming dumber with age.'

'Nonna was old. And she was ill, not dumb.'

'Isn't that the same thing?'

'It really isn't.'

Amelia started humming again as they crunched through leaves, the buzz of insects in the shade. Angela lost her for a second in a sudden patch of darkness, and she was forced to pick up her pace.

Of course she remembered it. She could remember the smallest detail of the most seemingly insignificant moments: a long July afternoon, and the murky water in the half-deflated pool; her mother breastfeeding her brother on the settee; her father washing the car. The rocky beach during summer holidays. The tear-jerking lyrics of that stupid, stupid song.

They re-emerged into the field: the grass was a vivid green, as if it had been painted. The tent shone in the sunlight. Angela narrowed her eyes and stopped.

'Something wrong?' asked Amelia.

'I just need to catch my breath. I've been a bit out of shape recently.'

'Of course, sorry. Give me that.' Amelia slipped the freezer bag's strap off her sister's shoulder and hefted it onto hers.

'Thank you.'

'No need to thank me.'

They put their things next to an isolated tree, a few yards from the stream, then unfolded the chairs and placed them next to each other. They went back to the tent in silence, blew up their air mattresses and rolled out their sleeping bags.

They almost hadn't spoken on the motorway, either, as they drove with the windows down, warm air hissing into the overheating car. At one point, Angela had rummaged in her bag. 'I forgot my sunglasses.'

'Is that a problem?'

'Well, yes – too much light is a little uncomfortable.'

Amelia had turned to look at her for a second, her hands firmly on the steering wheel, a field of corn behind her on the other side of the crash barrier, her hair dancing over her face like thin dark flames.

'I don't wear them,' she said. 'The light is so beautiful. I like things the way they are. Natural.'

'Is that why you never turn on the air conditioning?'

'That's the *worst*.'

'It's better than dying of heat.'

'You won't die, don't fret.' Amelia was squinting in the bright sunlight, her lips in a tight smile. She had the same face as her father, wide and square, the same light blue eyes. She had smiled at the tollbooth man, offering him her ticket and the money, saying: 'Have a good day.'

A rosary hung from the rear-view mirror. 'Where is this place anyway?' Angela had asked, looking at it. 'We're close to home now.'

'It's a surprise.'

'I don't want to go – home, I mean. I hope you didn't plan this with Mum and Daddy.'

'Of course not. I want to spend time with you.'

They took the turning before Rivafredda, passing a couple of sleepy towns in the lunchtime heat, and a small stable where a boy busy brushing a horse kept staring at the car. The road curved and then rose sharply, disappearing into the woods.

'I'm sure you'll love it, Angi. You'll see.'

You'll love it: that was it, end of discussion. Angela had sighed and given up.

The tent was dark blue, with a tiny window at the back and the open mouth of the entrance at the front.

'It always looks hard at the start,' Amelia said.

Angela thought about this for a second, then asked: 'What do you mean?'

'A lot of people think that pitching a tent is a big effort, that's all. But it isn't.'

'I wouldn't know how to do it again, not on my own.'

'You just learned how.'

'Outdoor life, huh? I still don't get what you see in it.'

'It makes me feel good to get away from the noise, and it's good for the children too. Is there anything better?'

'Only about a million other things.'

Angela looked towards the woods, the shining treetops, whose shadows crawled along the ground. She felt unsettled, as if panic were closing in (she knew it well) and was getting ready to knock at her door. Amelia said something else, so Angela looked at her and she seemed so much younger than her thirty-eight years, with those ridiculous walking boots, socks all the way up to her knees, a pair of shapeless shorts and a white vest top. A simple person, at peace with herself.

'I thought it'd be cooler,' said Angela, peeling her T-shirt from her back. 'We're quite far up.'

'It'll be different once the sun sets. You might even be cold tonight.'

'I'm used to that.'

Amelia turned around. 'You'll be fine then,' she replied; it sounded like a reproach, but she immediately broke back into a smile.

A thin cloud hung suspended over the trees.

'I need to wee,' Angela said.

Amelia pointed her towards a small wooded area of low, sparse pine trees, a little further down, and a dark rock that looked like an altar. 'Loo roll is in the plastic bag. And there's another bag you can use to throw it away, after.'

Angela started walking through the grass, panic already knocking at the door, then slid into the shade – *Please, not now* – and started fumbling with the button on her jeans.

She pushed them down to her ankles, pulled down her knickers and squatted: urine snaked through the dried pine needles.

'Everything okay, Angi?' Amelia shouted.

Still crouched down, her mouth bitter-tasting and filled with saliva, she whispered: 'Leave me alone.'

Three days earlier, completely drunk in a nightclub car park, she had been sick over her own shoes.

She'd got home in the middle of the night and dialled Amelia's number – a surprising choice to make, even to her. What had started in the car park, something she couldn't have predicted and still didn't really understand, had pushed her to break the silence.

'I'll be right there,' Amelia had replied, her voice sticky with sleep. 'Don't move.'

'Where would I go?'

After all, who else could she tell if not her sister? She had waited for her on the settee, smoking, in the desolation of the single room that was her flat, her sick-splattered shoes in the shower, still hearing the echo of the music that had been playing while she was throwing up, slamming against her back whenever someone had opened the door to the club.

She'd been sitting on a car bonnet, a horrible taste in

her mouth, when a voice behind her had said: 'Hey! You need to get off there.'

She had turned round slowly to see a young man leaning his elbow against the roof. His hand, pale in the darkness, held a keyring around one finger,

Angela had mumbled: 'Sorry.' He'd turned to his right and said: 'This one's really gone.' Standing on the passenger side was another young man. 'Yep, truly gone.'

A car's headlights had lit up the car park. Its tyres crunched on the tarmac, someone called out a last goodbye, then scattered laughter.

Angela had tried to stand up but had only been able to take one uncertain step before she'd fallen back onto the bonnet.

'Jesus fucking Christ, careful,' the voice of the first boy said.

She'd raised her head, looking at the field stretching beyond the car park and up to a line of trees, distant and dark in the night: the point where buildings, the city, started to rise. Darkness floated over the pale sheen of the streets of the town's outskirts.

Someone shouted: 'Wait for us!' then the door to the club, a concrete building next to a bingo hall, had slammed, muffling the sound of the band currently performing.

'Hey,' the voice said again. His keys were still looped around his finger. His face was long and thin.

'I'm going, I'm going,' Angela said, her words slow, slurred.

He gave a flick of his wrist; the keys jingled.

A group of young women walked across the car park towards the road. They were talking among themselves, holding each other's arms. Another car appeared out of the darkness and they lurched to one side and stopped. The car braked suddenly and someone asked: 'What's your plan now, loves?' and they giggled before setting off again. The car drove past them with a small toot.

The boy with the keys had moved away from the car roof and was now standing in front of the driver's door; he was keeping an eye on the group of girls, as if he knew them, or maybe planned on following them, then he pointed them out to his friend.

Angela stood up and the two men said something to each other; they were staring at her now. The friend was much taller than the car roof; in fact, he was so big that he didn't look like he could ever fit inside. He was wearing a tight T-shirt and a baseball cap that covered his eyes. What she noticed above all, though, was his hair, which was white and fine as lint, casually resting on his shoulders.

'Where's your car?' asked the boy with the keys. He had a scrawny neck and hollow cheeks, dark eyes.

His friend removed his cap, smoothed his white hair, then placed the cap back on his head.

'Well?' the boy insisted. 'Where's your car – are you going to tell me or not?'

There were still two cars in the furthest part of the car park. A group of people were talking loudly: they said goodbye to each other, piled into the cars and left. All that remained was a white van parked by the side of the road.

Angela shook herself. 'Where did everyone go?' she said. She looked at the club's open doors, the inside now bathed in light and empty. Only the band members were left, standing on the stage, poring over their instruments.

'So you don't have a car then?'

'I came with a guy.'

'And who is this *guy*?' the boy with the keys asked. 'Where did he go?'

She couldn't remember his name. 'What do I care?' she said. 'He was a pain in the arse.' Then she looked down at her shoes and started chuckling. 'Fuck, I was sick over myself. And I lost my bag. Someone took it.'

'Are you blind or something?' the boy with the cap said, reluctantly raising a hand to point at the car bonnet. 'It's right there.'

Angela saw the bag and started chuckling again. 'You saved my life,' she told him. 'You. Saved. My. Life.'

'What's your name?' asked the boy with the keys. He had moved closer, again that hollowed out face, and she noticed the flicker of a tattoo, like the black tail of a small animal, peeking out of the collar of his T-shirt.

'Angela. Fucking stupid name, right?'

'And how are you getting home, Angela?'

'I don't want to go home.' She shook her head vigorously. 'I was having fun.'

'So what do you want to do?'

'She probably has a phone, right?' said the boy with the cap. 'She can ask that guy to come and pick her up. Or we can call him.'

'Shut up, I'm talking to Angela.'

'It's none of our fucking business,' his friend replied. 'Not tonight.'

'She sat on *my* fucking car, so it's *my* fucking business. She was almost sick all over it.'

'Sorry, sorry, sorry,' Angela whined, and shoved her hands into her bag, looking for her cigarettes, and saw the band leave the club and cross the dark car park, instruments in hand, heading for the white van. 'They could've kept playing. The night isn't over yet,' she protested. The van's lights washed over the road and she waved her hand. Then she felt another hot wave of nausea rise inside her, and she suddenly bent over, holding her hair against the back of her neck.

'Oh shit,' one of the two young men exclaimed.

Angela spat, a rasping noise coming from her throat. 'It's okay, I'm okay. I want a smoke,' she said. 'I don't know where I put them.'

The boy with the keys fished a packet out of his back pocket, offered her one and lit it for her, looking her in the eye. She started laughing again, on the edge of the now empty car park.

At dawn, on the settee with her sister now next to her, the name of the guy who had driven her to the club came back to her: Sandro Lavatori.

'He works at the supermarket too. How could I forget his name?'

The previous afternoon, before the beginning of Angela's shift, they'd been making small talk until he cleared his throat and told her about the band playing that evening. 'We could go together, if you like.'

'I'd like that, yes.'

Sandro Lavatori was a large guy with hair thinning at the temples, perfectly at ease in his red apron behind the meat counter. They didn't really know each other, nor did she really like him, but sometimes he looked at her as if she were gorgeous – a delicate little thing, and not the pathetic, confused woman who took anti-anxiety meds and drank too much, and ended up in bed with whoever was available.

'So I'll come and pick you up – if you give me your address?'

As they were driving along a dark road, Sandro had told her that he was divorced: 'It didn't last long, just a couple of years. We stayed friends though. What about you?'

'What about me?'

'Uh, I don't know. Have you ever been married?'

'No,' Angela had said. She had thought of the bleeding meat at the butcher's counter. 'I have no one. I lost everyone.'

He had bought her first drink in the busy club, then her second and her third. 'Are you sure you're not overdoing it?'

The band was playing and she was laughing and drinking more, grinding against him. Then she had stepped into the middle of the dance floor and danced with someone else.

'I was a real bitch.'

'You didn't like him,' Amelia replied, her legs folded up underneath her. 'You just told me that.'

'I should've told him I had something else going on. Come up with an excuse, I dunno.'

Sandro Lavatori was a kind man, and he had followed her into the crowd of people, shouting over the music: 'What are you doing?' as if he felt sorry for her.

'I want to stay here,' she'd said.

'You can't even stay upright. Come on, let's get some fresh air.' He had held her wrist in the middle of the crowd: a light touch, just to guide her.

Angela had pushed him away, hitting him in the chest: 'Leave me alone, go away.'

In her flat, she dried her eyes. 'I was so mean to him.'

'These things happen.'

'Not to you they don't.'

'Which thing's don't?' Amelia asked her.

Making a scene in public. Insulting someone. Being sick all over a car park. Drifting away.

'Don't cry,' Amelia said. 'I'm here now. Tell me what happened after that.'

Angela had still been laughing, still clutching her cigarette, when she'd got into the car and had crumpled onto the back seat.

The boy with the keys had started the engine. 'Let's go then,' he'd said, but he hadn't driven off immediately. He was stroking the steering wheel with his thumbs, as if unsure about which direction to take.

The one with the cap looked shrivelled in the passenger seat; his huge arms were folded on his lap, his large knees pressed against the dashboard.

'Wait,' she'd stopped laughing. 'I don't even know your names.'

'We're your new best friends,' the boy with the keys had said, and the other one had glanced at him then turned around to face her, lifting the peak of his cap. That was when Angela had noticed he had no eyebrows – his arches were entirely naked, jutting out like those of a newborn baby. He had told her their names, which she hadn't been able to register: something had lurched slightly in her throat.

'Are you happy now?' the boy with the keys had asked. 'Flick your ash out of the car, please. I only had it cleaned this morning.'

'She reeks of sick, anyway,' the friend had said. 'That sort of smell always lingers.'

'Don't be a wanker, don't insult her.'

'I'm not insulting her,' his friend had replied, sliding his phone out of his pocket: a whiteish glow illuminated the inside of the car.

'Her again?' the boy with the keys had asked him. 'How many texts has she sent now?'

'What the fuck should I do? I've already told her.'

'Tell her to go fuck herself.'

Angela had wound down the window and chucked out the cigarette. After leaning back against the headrest, she'd closed her eyes, slipping into darkness, the boys' voices growing more and more distant as the car started to move.

When she returned to her sister, under that solitary tree, Amelia set up the coffee pot: 'It's quite something when made with fresh water from the stream,' she said. Light was wriggling through the branches, speckling the shadows with a slight iridescence.

Angela took out a cigarette and sat down. She removed her shoes, stretched out her skinny, jeans-clad legs and wiggled her toes inside her black socks.

'You should quit with those,' Amelia said. 'The cigarettes. You don't need them. It would help you with everything else too.'

'Please, don't start.'

'I don't want to start anything.'

'You used to smoke too.'

'When I was sixteen, Angi, and for a single summer.'

'You gave me my first one, remember? You enjoyed it too.'

One torrid afternoon, behind Bar Gioia, Amelia had requested one from the classmate she fancied back then

– long, curly hair, a bit of a bully – who lit it, and shoved it between Angela's lips. She had ordered her to inhale and then started laughing, watching her cough out smoke. 'She's such a mess,' Amelia had snorted. 'It looks like she's choking.' She stared, google-eyed, at her classmate. *She* was an expert, she was trying to imply, not a little girl like Angela, only fourteen and unable to inhale without spluttering and crying. The same little girl who used to burst into tears in the cupboard. Amelia had shaken her head, sighing. 'Let me smoke that.'

Later, on the way home, she had handed her a packet of chewing gum. 'Take it,' she'd said.

'I don't want any right now.'

'*Take it.* So Mum and Daddy don't notice the smell, stupid. Do I have to explain everything?'

Amelia looked at her, perplexed, as if she didn't remember any of this. 'I don't want a fight,' she said.

'Don't give me advice, then. And don't call me Angi.'

They heard the coffee bubbling. Amelia removed the pot from the camping stove, poured the coffee into the cups, took out a tin of sugar, and sat back down, stirring a teaspoonful into each cup.

'Sorry,' Angela said. 'I just can't stand it.'

Amelia shrugged imperceptibly. 'We used to come here often, with the children, when they were smaller. It doesn't take long to get here – as you saw – but it's a world to itself. They used to go skinny dipping.'

Angela imagined her nephews, the shouting and laughter rising up into the air. 'You too? Did you get naked too?' she asked.

'No. Of course not.'

'Why not?'

'I'd be so embarrassed.'

'I thought you enjoyed . . . how did you put it earlier? *Natural* things. You never used to overthink that kind of thing. You were never the shy one.'

'Of course I was.'

Angela could hear the water babbling in the stream behind them. Another cloud, she noticed, had joined the single cloud from earlier.

'I came back here by myself last summer,' Amelia said, staring at the coffee in her cup. 'I needed some time to think. It was a bad time, as you can imagine.'

Angela could imagine, yes. Hadn't she been the one, just two years earlier, to hurt Amelia by telling her: 'Don't come looking for me, you only make me feel worse'?

'And you weren't scared?' she asked.

'Of what?'

'Of being alone in a place like this. Isolated.'

'There's no need to be scared – there's no danger here. It's what we feel inside that matters. And God never leaves our side.'

'Great speech,' Angela remarked. She had a sudden craving for a drink. She looked at the tent; at that breathtaking clearing. She finished her cigarette, rubbed it through the grass, let it fall into her empty cup.

Later, Amelia handed her a sandwich: 'Do you mind if I say a couple of words?' She lowered her head and closed her eyes. 'Thank you for the food you have given us. Watch over us, Lord. Protect my sister who is here, with me.'

Angela whispered: 'Pretty sure he can see me.'

Amelia opened one eye, the blue of her iris moving from side to side, before saying: 'Amen.'

They ate in the shade.

'I made so many,' Amelia said, and she gestured at the sandwiches in the freezer bag. 'You'll have to finish them all.'

They put the used tinfoil into the plastic bag and took off their socks; a light wind was blowing, and they lay down barefoot on the grass.

'I missed you,' Amelia said, and then she dozed off, her mouth slightly open.

Lying on her side, Angela watched her sleep. The stupid song that her sister had sung earlier suddenly popped back into her head – it told the depressing story of a young woman married to a whaler who drowned at sea. Their mother had often sung it to them when they were younger.

She rolled onto her back. The clouds were darker over the wooded area, but the blue sky still flashed between the branches. She thought of Mass, which Amelia attended every Sunday with her husband and children and which – she had told Angela again, on the settee in her studio flat – had been the light that had saved her, the endless source of joy and hope. 'Jesus's sacrifice makes any suffering bearable,' she'd said, her fingers knotted on her lap, her gaze flitting between the bin overflowing with bottles, the piles of dirty plates in the sink, and a wilted orchid next to the TV. 'I want to help you, Angi. Please, tell me what happened.'

'I just need to sleep.'

Everyone loved Amelia, because she was strong and kind and thoughtful. She had been so *brave*. And now she was dozing, snoring lightly.

Amelia at sixteen, a cigarette between her lips, who had enjoyed bringing Angela to tears in front of her bully of a classmate, making doe-eyes at him, blowing out smoke.

She ripped out a handful of grass, squeezed it in her fist, let it fall back onto the ground. That's what she was thinking about: a glimpse of the old resentment. Then she turned onto her other side, stretched out an arm, shoved her hand into her bag. Found her anti-anxiety meds.

She went back to looking at the sky – brief flashes through the leaves – as the bitterness of the pill filled her mouth. Behind her eyelids, as soon as she closed her eyes, she suddenly saw an unknown bedroom, the breeze wafting a small curtain. A naked man with his legs spread wide lying next to her. Angela finishing off a bottle, then trying to stand up and sway her hips, wearing only her knickers, asking him: 'Enjoying the show?'

Let me out. Don't leave me here.

The man was saying: 'You look ridiculous.'

That was how she slipped into sleep.

It was as though their brother's death – all the pain and desperation of it – had made Amelia imperturbable, blunting the downside of everything, smoothing her like a pebble. She often talked about the light that had started shining in the darkness: she'd say she could see it. 'It's such a beautiful light, Angi. I'm sure He was there with him, in those final moments.'

Angela had wanted to slap her. 'He was alone, Amelia.'

Her sister had replied with a light smile, a shrug of the shoulders. 'And how can you be so sure?'

Amelia had married during her PhD in Biology. She had married the boy who had shown up – one late September morning in 1989 – in Cave and had loaded her suitcase into his car, taking her back to the city.

The day of her thesis discussion she had been very obviously pregnant. That evening, at the head of the restaurant table, her father had asked what her plans were.

'I want to take care of the baby,' she'd said.

'Of course. But I was talking about work.'

'It doesn't matter to me any more.'

A shadow of surprise had run across his face: 'It doesn't matter?'

'No.'

'You've always wanted to teach, like me. You'd be an excellent teacher.'

'There are more important things,' Amelia had said. 'What do you think, Mum?'

Sara had been wearing her Sunday best, but her lips were cracked and her eyes puffy. She had muttered: 'Take me home, Pietro. I'm tired.'

'Amelia, please,' he had insisted. 'Please reconsider. You're too smart.'

'Can we change the subject?' Angela had poured herself another glass of wine. 'She'll do whatever she wants to do, Daddy. It's not that big a loss, you should know that. We're experts in big losses, we are.' She had already missed two exam seasons and the following year she would go on to drop out of university altogether.

Her father had given her a long, disapproving look. 'This isn't funny.'

Half an hour later, in the small garden behind the restaurant, when her brother-in-law had come to find her – 'Do you want a coffee? Are you still smoking?' – Angela had blurted out whether he thought that, in fact, either sister would do; whether he wanted to try the other one out for a change.

'I've always kind of fancied you,' she'd said, stroking his cheek.

'How much have you had to drink?'

'Not enough.' She had rested her arms on his shoulders.

Amelia's shape had materialised against the darkness, holding her belly, and Angela had stepped back. Her sister had joined them, taking them both by the arm: 'It's so lovely out here, isn't it?'

Angela had hated her for her full cheeks, her round belly and breasts, her unnatural calm. As they took her back to the student accommodation that she would soon leave, Amelia had mentioned a prayer group that met every Tuesday at the church where they'd got married.

'We've been a couple of times, and I really think we'll keep going. The priest is fantastic. You should meet him, Angi.'

'Yes, you'd like him,' her brother-in-law had added.

Amelia had turned to look at her: that smooth, polished pebble. 'Once the baby's born, that'll be medicine for Mummy, too. Everything will be different.'

They slept for over an hour. When they woke up, the sky was stained with grey clouds. They sat up, looking at it.

'I don't think it's going to get worse,' Amelia said. 'The forecast was good.'

Angela smoked a cigarette and her sister put on some more coffee.

'Tell me about the kids,' Angela said. A streak of light rested on her face.

'What do you want to know?'

'Anything.'

'Well, they're growing so fast.' Amelia nibbled the inside of her cheek. 'You could stay with us for a little bit, tomorrow afternoon. They'd be happy to see you. Then I can take you home.'

'Do you think you'll have more?'

'It's . . . they're not coming,' Amelia replied, looking over at the woods, as if she could see the children lined up on the grass, waiting for her to join them. She shooed away a fly, then looked at Angela out of the corner of her eye. 'Two years,' she said.

'Yes, I know.'

'I just want to know what's going on – what have I done to you?'

The panic crept closer again – a nail of terror scratching at the door – as the leaves bristled in the wind. Amelia brought her hands together and closed her eyes, shifting in her camping chair: Angela thought she was praying.

Instead, she said, 'I came to your place. The supermarket too. I needed to see you.'

'Really?'

'You never noticed me?'

'No.'

'The last time I came, there was a woman with a crying child, sitting in the trolley,' Amelia said. 'You were trying to make him laugh. She was hysterical, almost about to strangle him.'

Angela could not remember: 'So many people come through,' she said. Legions of hysterical mothers and crying children.

'You succeeded – he stopped crying. You've always been good at these things.'

'What things?'

'The ones that really matter.'

'Are you fucking kidding me?'

'No, I mean it. I was always jealous.' Amelia frowned and closed her eyes, as if trying to bring something back from the past. 'When we were younger and our brother cried or Mum looked tired, you dropped everything and went to help. Mum used to say you had a big heart. I think so too.'

'Oh, give it up. I know that's not true.'

'I'd just like you to know how much I've missed you.'

Don't call me, Amelia, don't come looking for me. I want to be alone.

Angela stood up and turned her back on her sister. She walked to the tent, feeling the grass under her bare feet and a sweet, sticky liquid rising in her chest, in her throat, that could easily have suffocated her. Then she walked back.

'It makes me so fucking angry,' she said.

'What does?'

'The way you are.'

Amelia looked at her, then stood up herself. 'It's not worth it,' she said. 'Let's go for a walk, instead.'

'Where?'

She had woken up on the back seat of that unknown car and mumbled, 'Where am I?' She could see houses and lights still on. A petrol station with a yellow sign.

The boy with the keys had glanced in the rear-view mirror. 'You looked like you were dead.'

'I fell asleep.'

'You can do what you want, you're among friends here.'

There was something surprisingly genuine in that reply, and Angela forgot that she hadn't given him her address; nor did she ask herself where they were taking her.

The boy with the cap was looking out of the window; his phone lit up again and he glanced at the screen, read something, started typing.

'Is that your girlfriend?' she asked.

He shook his head. The white glow made his features even sharper under the peak of his cap.

'I think she is.'

'You're right, Angela,' the boy with the keys said. 'They were made for each other, that's why he shagged her.'

'This is none of her business,' said the boy with the cap.

'Angela is our friend, now. We tell her everything.'

They stopped at a red light. The boy with the keys stretched an arm out of the window and touched the roof of the car – another tattoo darkened his elbow, as if he'd dipped it in ink.

Angela could hear his fingers tapping. 'I want a tattoo as well,' she said.

'What do you want to get?'

'I don't know.'

'You need to think about it properly. You can never take it off. It's like branding.'

'I'd never get one, not even if they paid me,' said the boy in the cap.

'We didn't ask for your opinion, did we, Angela?'

She said: 'I read this quote somewhere.' She let her head fall back against the upholstery. The air was cool on her sweaty skin. '*Everything is imagined.* I could get that tattooed.'

They stayed silent for a bit.

'The fuck does it mean, everything is imagined?' asked the boy in the cap. They were driving through a town centre: the car turned left onto a long straight road, between fields and warehouses. 'I once saw a guy walking a chicken on a lead,' he added, as if this was a natural follow-on. 'He talked to it too, I swear; he'd given it a name and everything. Some people, huh?'

Angela leaned between the front seats. 'Where are we going now?' she asked, and the one driving briefly lifted his fingers from the steering wheel.

'Wherever you want,' he replied.

'I don't think I know where we are.'

'Nowhere.'

Her mind was buzzing – the stubborn bumping of an insect against a glass pane. She rubbed her temples, made a face, then covered her mouth with her hand. 'I think I'm about to be sick again,' she said.

He pulled over immediately: 'Get out.' There was no kindness in his voice now.

Angela felt for the handle, got out of the car and moved a couple of steps away. She brushed her hair from her face, leaning forward. When the retching stopped, she wiped her mouth and looked up: the skeleton of a building, all pillars and planks, planted in the middle of a field. She heard the puttering of the engine on the empty road.

The boy with the keys leaned his head out of the window. 'Do you want to be left here?' he asked. 'Get a move on.'

The passenger door opened and the boy with the cap got out. 'You better get back inside,' he said. Then he lowered his voice: 'He hates waiting.' He took off his cap, toyed with it in the dark.

'You saved me,' she said. 'It was you.'

He sighed, and Angela took a lock of his white hair in her fingers. 'Light hurts you, right? I've never seen someone like you before. What's it called? I can't remember the word.'

He looked at her hand, his eyes quizzical beneath the naked brow. 'Get back in the car,' he said.

Angela threw herself into the back seat again and the car screeched off down the road.

'You really had fun tonight, huh?' the boy with the keys said. 'And you must have really pissed him off, that guy, if he just left you there. But us two are different, don't worry. We won't leave a girl like you all by herself. We'll take her wherever she wants to go. And we'll let her have fun.'

Cap boy shot him a look.

'How old are you two?' Angela asked.

'Guess.'

'Old enough to drive – or you are, at least.'

'No shit.'

Cap boy said: 'I drive much better – my feet are more sensitive. It's like an instinct.'

The other shook his head. 'Load of bollocks.'

She suddenly realised, almost shuddering at the thought, that they might be brothers, even though there was no resemblance.

'I have a sister,' she said. 'We're not talking.'

'She doesn't understand you?' the boy with the keys said. He sucked some air through his teeth. 'No one understands you, do they? Except us. Never let them trick you, trust me. They're all out to trick you.'

Angela put a hand out of the window, then pulled it back in and rubbed it over her face. She would've liked to add: 'I had a brother, too.' She would've liked to start drinking again. She suddenly felt the weight of her thirty-six years. God, she was pathetic, she thought. She looked outside again, at the blinking traffic light, a yellow sign for a petrol station. She said: 'We've already been here.'

The boy with the keys pulled a cigarette out of the packet, lit it, took a drag, and handed it to her: 'Take it.'

Cap boy's phone lit up again; he didn't even look at it, he just switched it off and thrust it into one of his pockets.

'I just had an idea,' the other one said. He looked like he was talking with his mouth closed. 'Let's go and pick her up too, then she can stop calling, and you can be all over her again. What do you say, Angela? Are you getting bored, all alone back there? There are so many places we could go to, the four of us, and—'

'Why don't you shut the fuck up?' cap boy interrupted. His hair looked like cotton against the dark headrest. 'You know why I did it. I don't even remember her face.'

'You gave her your number, though.'

'No I didn't – she must have asked around for it, I dunno. Anyway, it's off now. So just drop it.'

The boy with the keys slowly wagged his index finger between the seats. 'Nuh-uh, I don't think so. I've barely started.'

'I should be getting home,' Angela said.

'Don't you fucking start. I'm driving you around for free. I'm not a taxi, I need to have some fun too.'

Cap boy turned around to stare at her: his face, white and naked, was covered in a film of sweat. He turned back to look at his friend and put a hand on his shoulder, but the one driving jerked away: 'Don't touch me.' He accelerated, then suddenly slammed on the brakes, and the car zig-zagged on the dark road. It ended up half on the verge, with only the rear still on the tarmac.

Cap boy hit his head on the roof. 'What the fuck are you doing?'

The boy with the keys turned off the engine, leaving the headlights on.

Angela had slid to the edge of the seat. She looked up at the windscreen: through it, a grassy field dotted with small trees. The air was dark and thick. The one at the steering wheel said again, 'I need to have some fun.' He was still talking through gritted teeth. He got out, slamming the door behind him, lit another cigarette and started walking across the grass, beyond the headlights.

Cap boy said: 'Crap.'

The burning dot moved further into the darkness.

Angela looked at the empty road behind her: an endless valley, weeds growing on either side of the road. There was no one around to ask for help. 'I don't want to be here,' she whined, as if the car were the cupboard of her childhood, the damp cellar. She pushed her back against the car door and hugged her knees.

'Neither do I,' cap boy replied. He removed his cap and put it on the dashboard, then ran his hand through his hair. 'You shouldn't have come. We've been getting in a lot of trouble recently.'

'Trouble?'

The burning dot disappeared among the small trees. Then it reappeared, and she realised she had been holding her breath.

'Can you tell me where we're going?'

'You'll see soon enough,' Amelia replied.

They walked a little further up the mountain, through the woods, reaching a clearing that gave them a view over the valley below: the snaking river, Rivafredda and Cave. The Ponte shopping centre, which when they were younger had been a cotton mill.

Amelia raised her arm and pointed. 'That's our house down there. That's the hospital. Daddy's school.'

'You do remember I also used to live here, don't you?'

'And there, more or less, is the beach.'

The gravelly car park. The short, shaded path that led to the river and the small island, covered in reeds, in the middle of the current. It had been their favourite place, once. Angela pictured it in front of her, with vivid clarity: the wet pebbles and the glimmering of the water, her brother swimming.

'Those two boys, remember them?' Amelia said. 'Kissing on that flat stone, at the end of the beach. It just came back to me.' She stretched her lips into a wide smile. 'What did we used to call it?'

'The bench.'

Amelia nodded.

'He was, what, seven or eight? He shot off towards them and stood there, staring.'

The two boys had pulled away from each other – at the time, Angela used to think, love between two boys, or two girls, wasn't something you should show in public.

She pulled her hair back in the warm wind. She flicked her tongue over her teeth: the shiver of anxiety of that memory, like a too-tight cap squeezing her head.

'Well, Daddy dragged him away by the arm,' she said. 'Physically removed him.'

'He did not,' Amelia protested.

'He very much did.'

'He just told him not to bother them.'

The two boys were both students of his, their father had said that evening. Angela had heard him talk to their mother, and what he had seen at the beach had obviously bothered him – he'd called it '*that* kind of behaviour'.

'He was just looking at them, Amelia,' she said, and shut her eyes. When she reopened them and turned towards her sister, Amelia had let her arms fall to her sides: 'Daddy never hurt him,' she said.

'There are many different ways to hurt someone.'

'Such as? Go on, tell me.'

'He never made any effort to understand him.'

'And you did?'

The sun shone briefly over the tiny cars driving up and down the road along the river.

'We were a nice family,' Amelia added, brushing her hair out of her face. She held the whole valley in her gaze. 'We're still a family. Mum and Daddy would be so happy if you dropped in at home, or even just called them. Believe it or not, we all still care about you. We talk about you, and we're concerned.'

'Then stop.' Angela had rolled her eyes. What she didn't say was that her heart was crumbling, that the cap was pressing against her temples. And that she was certain – she remembered it very clearly – her brother had burst into tears that day.

'Do you want to walk a bit further?' Amelia asked.

'I want to go back.'

They sat back under the tree, its leafy branches rustling. Amelia phoned her husband, talked to her children, wished them goodnight. She went to the stream and filled a bottle with water, opened the freezer bag and handed Angela two more sandwiches. She said her prayer – 'Protect us, O Lord' – and they had dinner.

The sun was setting.

Angela moved her chair to face the stream. She had taken another pill in secret and her body was now relaxing into a light sleepiness. 'That song,' she said. Their mother had taught it to their brother, too, when he was still a child, and he used to hum it to himself constantly. Angela could hear his young voice drifting from somewhere in the house: *E lei piangendo l'accompagnò sul molo*. 'I remember it,' she continued. She crossed her legs, studied the sole of her shoe. 'I used to like it. Now I find it unbearable.'

'It was just a song.'

'It was depressing. A guy dies at sea, yay. And yet Mum always seemed so happy, always in good spirits. But maybe that wasn't true.'

'What do you mean?'

'We've been pretending everything was fine, but something was always wrong.'

'People are people,' Amelia said. 'They're not black or white.'

'It would be better if they were.'

Amelia fell quiet for a moment, then suddenly she said harshly: 'You really do think you have all the answers, don't you?' She stared fixedly ahead. 'You think everyone else is blind or stupid.'

When she looked back at the stream again, Angela realised it was almost dark. 'At least I'm not trying to fool myself,' she replied. 'At least I don't try to hide. That rosary in the car – you want to carry your Jesus around with you? You really think it helps?'

'That's none of your concern.'

'It's just a question.'

Amelia rubbed her hands on her shorts. 'It's *never* just a question,' she said. 'Not with you.'

'Okay then. Go on, spit it out, say what you really think. Spit out all of your anger, like you always did.'

'I never did.'

Little venomous snake, Angela thought. 'Oh yes you did. You did. You used to shove me in that cupboard, and you thought it was hilarious. You were *nasty*.'

Amelia stood up: Angela saw her legs rising up next to her.

'Nasty? It was all your fault: you were always in my way. "Don't leave me, Amelia. Take me with you, Amelia. I want to come too." Always with those puppy-dog eyes. And Mum would force me to bring you along, because you were all alone, you *poor thing*. But I know what you're really like.'

Angela was still watching the water, her face relaxed, but this made her frown. 'What are you talking about?'

'The list is too long.'

'Start listing then.'

'That boy I fancied, at school. He was the one who told me, did you know that?' Amelia said. 'He told me you kissed him. And I didn't believe him, but then that day I came home, I came into your room, and your face, your face was just—'

Angela could feel her temples pulsing. 'That's not what happened.'

Amelia had reached the stream; she picked up a rock and chucked it into the water, then turned around. 'Do you want to know why I never told you?' Her face, in the sunset, was a dying light. She raised her hands. 'I always hoped you'd be the one to tell me.'

'Should I go and confess? Say a little prayer?'

'It wouldn't hurt.'

'So I can end up like you? All that crap about hope, about joy. There is no joy. Our brother stole from other people's homes. He scared them to death and then he topped himself. While *we* were sleeping. And we have no idea what was wrong with him.'

'And you think that drinking and popping pills isn't hiding?'

Angela shook her head.

'No? What about going around shagging anything with a pulse?'

'He was the one who kissed me, Amelia. I was a child.' She felt as if she had an ice cube in her mouth and her sister was forcing her to bite it. 'I wasn't like you. You knew how to do these sorts of things.'

'See? Never your fault.'

Angela had thought about that moment often, the afternoon when she'd bumped into that bully and he had offered her a sip of his Coke and asked her: 'Do you want to go for a walk?' Like a tear that needed to be quickly patched up. She had kept the secret – or what she thought was a secret – until her brother's death, after which everything lost any meaning.

'What do you want me to tell you? That I wasn't expecting it and that I liked it? It was my first time. I told him no, because I was your sister, and he started laughing. He was laughing at both of us, do you understand?'

Amelia clapped her hands very, very slowly. 'Little Angi,' she said.

Then they felt the first raindrops, as big as coins and cold. A second later, the heavens opened.

Amelia yelled: 'We need to get inside the tent,' and Angela saw her take a step in her direction, offering her a hand, but then she slammed her arms down by her sides and disappeared off into the rain.

Alone, Angela removed her T-shirt and chucked it into the darkness. 'Fuck everything,' she muttered.

Still sitting on her camping chair, she threw back her head, opened her mouth and stuck out her tongue, at one with the rush of the wind and the dull roar of the rain.

Angela could feel the air blowing in from the open window pushing against the back of her head, almost like an elastic surface that she could no longer cross.

She could see the shadow of the boy with the keys moving across the field, beyond the headlight beams, the burning tip of his cigarette.

Cap boy slammed his fists onto his knees. 'Sometimes I think he's out of his mind,' he said. 'Just like that guy with the chicken. He wants to keep me on a lead.'

'Your girlfriend . . .' she whispered, then didn't know how to continue.

'I was off my face, that time.' Cap boy looked at her out of the corner of his eye. 'And he was furious – said he never wanted to see me again. That's what he's like. But at the end of the day we're the same. We grew up in the same shite. You know what I mean?'

Angela said yes, she did know.

'There's nothing you can do. You have to find someone who gets you, in all that shite,' he added. He stretched an arm out through the seats and took her hand: his fingers were thick and clammy. She whimpered.

The boy with the keys was kicking the grass; he chucked away his cigarette and squatted down on the ground.

'His dad used to beat him up, constantly – he said he was disgusted by him,' cap boy said. 'I would've gone over to kill that piece of shit. That's why he was furious. Instead I fucked it up, and I told him as much.'

Angela felt his fingers tighten their grip on her palm. 'Why did he hit him?' she asked.

'You still don't get it?' he said. He slipped down the seat and was forced to open his legs. 'When I was younger, people used to say I looked like a worm, or they'd call me "tighty whitey". Sometimes they hit me, and not just because of what I looked like. They used to call me a little poof. And I'd let them; I was different back then. Now I'd do their faces in.'

Angela could see him, big and strong, punching some-one in the face, mashing it into a bloody, soggy mask. *Have you had enough yet?*

'But you're a nice man,' she squeaked.

He clicked his tongue. 'There's nothing nice here.' He let go of her hand and touched his forehead. 'You know what I'm thinking? I'm thinking I don't give a toss about you. Up to me? You'd still be in that car park. I don't give a fuck about anyone, except him.' He reached across and switched off the headlights.

Angela asked him to switch them back on. 'What are you going to do?'

Cap boy didn't reply. He simply got out of the car, headed into the darkness and joined his friend.

She pulled herself away from the door, picked up her bag and went to open the clasp, her eyes fixed on the grass, her heart in her throat. She saw cap boy picking his friend up off the grass, the friend squirming, shouting: 'You want to shag this one too?' Then they fell silent, standing facing each other as if deciding on how to divide their prey. Cap boy raised his arms, put them around the other boy's waist and pulled him to him. They started kissing. It was a desperate kiss, Angela thought: she could almost hear their teeth clacking against each other, their tongues pushing.

You still don't get it?

After a moment, it was hard for her to make them out. She still had the impression that cap boy's white hair was glowing in the dark.

She saw them pulling away from each other, undoing their belt buckles and stripping off their tops and vests. Cap boy fell to his knees to kiss the other boy's chest, then he turned towards the road and gestured at the car.

They disappeared into the trees.

Angela let herself fall back into the seat, and her breathing slowly became steady again.

No cars drove by, and in the silence she thought she could hear the moans of the two boys crossing the endless valley, along with her breathing.

In the end, they'd given her a lift home. She didn't really know how long they'd been out for. During the drive back, cap boy kept his hand on the other boy's knee. The boy with the keys kept looking in the rear-view mirror, but every time he met Angela's eye he immediately looked away.

She watched cap boy's white hair on the dark headrest: it looked like a new life, still immaculate. A promise piercing the darkness, despite everything, headed who knew where.

'We're almost there,' she told them, when they got close to her building. She thanked them both for the lift and apologised for bothering them.

'Quite the evening, huh?' said the boy with the keys.

Cap boy nodded, as the light from the lampposts bounced off his white skin. Then he said: 'It was my birthday yesterday.' He started humming one of the songs that the band at the club had played on the creaky wooden stage.

'Happy birthday,' she said. 'Did you do anything special?'

He turned to his partner, then to look at her, his eyes wide under their naked brows. 'You know. You were there too.'

The clouds parted over the woods, on the other side of the stream, and Angela saw a small patch of stars appear. The rain eased off and then ceased entirely.

Amelia left the tent and joined her. She handed her a towel, and picked up her muddy, soggy T-shirt to rinse it in the stream.

'No one asked you to,' Angela said.

'It's nothing.'

Against the backdrop of trees along the opposite bank, Amelia immersed the T-shirt, scrubbed at the mud, wrung it out and draped it over her knee. Then she splashed her face. 'I needed that,' she said.

Angela hugged herself; her hair lay flat against her head, her jeans and bra were soaked and she was shivering. Her sister laid the T-shirt out over the freezer bag and said, 'You could've come inside the tent.'

'I didn't want to be in there with you.'

'Because I'm too nasty?'

'You're too nice.'

Amelia sat down; she probably hadn't slept either, Angela thought. 'It's still dark,' she said, as if her sister wouldn't have noticed. 'But it's almost morning.' There was a smell of wet soil around them, as something colder rose up from the stream.

Angela was silent.

'I'm not nice, you were right,' Amelia said, and Angela watched her blue eyes wander all around them. 'Sometimes I yell when the children won't listen. I yell, I cry, I make a scene.'

The outdoor life. Mass every Sunday. The shining light, joy and hope.

'I don't know what I'm saying, sorry.' Amelia straightened her back and smiled again. 'We need to move on, try and be better. You need to let sadness slide off you.'

Angela suppressed her laughter. 'Move on,' she repeated. 'You want to know something? I think Daddy had an affair that year.'

'What are you talking about?'

'I'd gone home, one weekend. February or March, I can't remember. And he had a mark, here, on his neck. He was trying to cover it. Whoever it was, they'd sucked pretty hard. I'd say that's moving on, right?'

Amelia's eyes narrowed; her lips were taut and thin. That was when Angela asked herself – and the thought stunned her – if her sister had suspected it too. 'I should've told you about it,' she continued, 'but you wouldn't have listened to me. You're like peas in a pod, you and Daddy. You're *perfect*.'

She remembered how, that day on the beach, as the two boys who'd been kissing had left, Amelia had simply continued to lie in the sun.

They both stared at a point in the distance, then Amelia brought her index finger to her mouth and tapped it against her lips. 'Now I get it,' she said.

'What?'

'Why you called me.' She sounded as if she had climbed a slope and could now see the view. 'Is there something else you want to tell me, maybe? Another little secret?'

'No,' Angela replied.

'Nothing happened to you, did it, the other night?' Amelia said. 'I thought you needed my help, but you were just drunk, that's all. Alone. You wanted someone to join you for your pity party. Same as always.'

Angela's heart blazed. 'Shut up,' she said. She leaned over from the chair and hit Amelia on the knee. For a moment she was still, then she began to flail around blindly, trying to hit her again. It was the first time she had ever done anything like this.

Amelia jumped backwards, held her by the wrists: 'Enough!' She pulled her sister's shaking hands towards her. Then, suddenly, as she was trying to hold her, she started sobbing. 'I think about him all the time, about how unhappy he must have been. I could've done something. Why didn't he tell me anything?'

'Because you were always the good one. Fuck. You never did anything wrong. What was he supposed to tell you?'

'Of course I did things wrong.'

Angela freed her hands: 'Let me go.' She looked at the wooded area where she had gone to relieve herself the previous day: the shining treetops, the still-dark grass, soaked in rain. 'You were always so selfish,' she said. 'Everything revolved around you.'

Daddy's girl. The favourite child. She's so smart.

Amelia, still sobbing, lowered her head. Neither of them said anything more for some time.

In that silence, Angela slipped into a daydream: far away from the isolated tree and the tent, she moved along the road in her mind, headed home and finally saw her brother's eyes, during his last summer, fixed on the woods behind the shadow of the garage. He'd head over there often when he wasn't in his room or wandering around town.

'At least I tried to help him, to understand something about him,' Angela said. 'He was like me.' She had joined him one day; sat down next to him and asked: 'What's going on? What's up with you?'

That's when it hit her, completely out of the blue, as she realised for the first time that things had not happened the way she remembered. The shot widened, until it was showing her entire room, Amelia knocking at the door and Angela, on the bed, felled by the heat, replying: 'Come in.'

'I'm going to go and talk to him for a second, Angi. Maybe I can get something out of him. Do you want to come with me?'

'No, I don't feel like it right now.'

It wasn't her who'd sat down next to him that day, trying to get some answers out of him. The following week, he had broken into Gemma's house with a screwdriver. Then he'd locked himself in the garage and started the car engine.

'It was you,' Angela said. 'I didn't lift a finger.'

Her sister frowned, but didn't ask her to explain what she meant. All she said, through the last of her sobs, was 'I'm tired.' She dried her face with her palms.

The sky looked like a freshly painted ceiling, the blue a little too vivid. It was going to be a glorious day.

'Same,' Angela said. She would've liked a smoke, but her bag was drenched and so, most likely, were its contents: cigarettes and lighter, her white pills. 'I didn't mean to hit you earlier. Or maybe I did.'

Amelia said that she knew what it was like to lose control, that it happened. 'But I don't really feel like staying – I'd like to get back to the children. Is that okay?'

'You thought this might go a bit better, didn't you?'

They exchanged a long look – yes of course, after two years of radio silence, yes. After all, was there anything wrong in hoping that something would go well? *The fore-cast was wrong*: that would be a better choice for a tattoo.

Amelia got up, folded up her chair and handed Angela her T-shirt. 'I can lend you a dry one, and a pair of shorts. I always bring a change of clothes.' After a second, she narrowed her eyes again. 'The thing about Daddy: we're not talking about it ever again.'

'Agreed.'

'He and Mum stayed together, in their own way. And they're getting old. Whatever happened, it happened a long time ago.'

In the still-damp air of the woods, Angela ruffled her hair.

'Do you want some breakfast, before we head back?' Amelia asked.

'No, thank you.' But that didn't mean she wasn't hungry. Everyone has their hunger. She had always been hungry, for affection, for attention, ever since she was a child. Wasn't it to sate her hunger that she'd let Amelia lock her in the cupboard?

'Would you like to do something with me?' she asked, pointing at the stream, the frothing water under the clear sky.

'A swim? You want to go in the water?'

Angela shrugged. 'Why not?'

'I don't have my swimsuit. I didn't think to bring it.'

'That makes two of us.'

Without waiting for an answer, Angela undressed and dumped her jeans, bra and knickers on the chair. She had a sudden, unexpected feeling of sweetness, the same kind she'd had when she'd relaxed, in the dark, on the back seat of the car, watching the two boys kiss.

As she stood there naked, Amelia stared at her: small red patches had bloomed over her cheeks and neck, maybe from the crying, or surprise – or maybe embarrassment. She cast a quick glance at the stream, biting her lip. 'Why not,' she said eventually, and undressed too. Angela took in her heavy breasts, her belly crisscrossed with white stretch marks. She carefully folded her clothes and placed them on top of her sister's. 'Let's go,' she said.

The water was cold enough to sting.

They lowered their hands and feet into it, giggling with disbelief. Then they waded in further. Eventually they were holding hands – who had taken the other's hand first? – carefully moving down the slippery bed, where it was possible to crouch down.

Amelia threw her head back. 'It almost feels warm, once you get used to it,' she said.

Angela thought it was true – it was true of many things, in fact – as the glare of the sun hurt her eyes, just like that clear sky so far away.

Sitting between them, their brother was quiet, looking at the woods, the brilliant green of the leaves: Angela could imagine it. She pictured three camping spots in the summer morning, all lined up next to each other.

Amelia stroked her shoulder. 'This was a very good idea of yours.'

'You were the one who brought me here.'

'Because I love you.'

'I know.'

'I want things to be better between us.'

And then Angela told her what had happened on the night she'd phoned her – her fear at first, and then the sweetness. The boy with the keys and the one with the cap. Amelia just smiled. When she finished her story, a thought came to Angela: *Protect my sister.* This is silly, she told herself. *Protect her and our brother, our parents, whoever you are, whatever it is you're doing.*

She dipped her mouth into the water and took a long cold drink, then whispered: 'You were there too.'

'Sorry?'

We were all there. Drunkenly partying and dancing with someone in the middle of the room – or maybe alone, with our back to the wall, waiting to sneak away and never come back. But we were there. And we're still there – shocking, I know – despite everything, there's no reason that it should be over.

Boy

Before

The house was empty, hidden by a small wooded area: no one had seen him climb over the gate, that time, and walk across the courtyard. The kitchen had a slight odour of burnt toast. The large dark rock, which his arm had thrown through the glass door, had ended up by the fridge, shards of glass across the floor. The morning light on the opposite wall.

He walked around, stopping to listen several times. He thumbed through a few books, rummaged in a few drawers and a couple of cupboards. He tried on a jacket that was hanging on a coat rack in the hall and looked at himself in the mirror. 'And who are you supposed to be?' he asked his reflection, in a hint of half-light. 'What, you don't want to answer me?' He put the jacket back and sat down on the settee, taking in his surroundings: framed photographs on a low piece of furniture, the stereo system, the paintings on the walls.

He had stood up, slowly, and headed upstairs.

It's a hot night, in the heart of summer.

Lying on his bed, he often thinks about that morning in July: the quiet house, the glass door at the back, the large dark rock. He felt like he'd imagined them, or that the person who threw the rock, who wandered through those rooms and eventually climbed back over the gate, picked up the bike from the woods and quickly pedalled away hadn't been him but another boy, instead. One that looked like him.

Now he walks along the path, moving from one side of the spine of dusty weeds to the other, his hood up and his hands deep in his pockets. The full moon lights his way through the woods all around him. It's two in the morning, but it could easily be dawn. He picks up a branch, slender and almost weightless, and waves it in the air – the crack of a whip – and throws it towards a clump of trees. The rough path looks like a dried-up stream, carved by water who knows how long ago, straight and deep as a cut along the hill's slope. The hem of a cloud brushes against the white halo of the moon.

He listens to his breathing, step after step. He is moving further and further from home, from his bedroom, from his parents and his sisters, as if someone were forcing him to march with a gun to his head. There is no going back. He stops for just a moment to catch his breath in the grassy clearing at the top of the hill. He raises his hands to the sky almost as if saying sorry, shivering despite the heat, a film of sweat on his neck and his heart slamming in his throat. There's a large pine tree in the lake of grass, dipped in the moon's brightness. A little further ahead is a trailer eaten up by rust, next to a pile of cracked logs.

He folds his arms, presses them against his ears and says: 'Move,' in a cruel voice he barely recognises. 'Get a fucking move on.'

He follows the edge of the clearing towards another cluster of trees pressed against each other like a gathering of people. Then he slips into the woods through the undergrowth and the thorns, into the densest spot; he gets caught on everything, and he jerks his arms away. Now the brightness has dimmed, as if clouded by steam or smoke. He reaches a small dip filled with dry leaves and broken branches, and tests the ground with the tip of his trainer to make sure he doesn't slip.

At last the metal roof glints in the dark, under the shadow of a chestnut tree: the shack. The walls are little more than rough, splintered wooden planks; inside are pieces of furniture and plywood panels stolen from a building site – a farmhouse being renovated – one night in June, carried here on his shoulders, three trips back and forth. Everything nailed together using his father's hammer, taken from the toolbox in the garage and shoved into his rucksack while his dad was at the school, busy with the national exams.

He climbs back up the side of the dip as if resurfacing; the ground is muddy under the dry leaves.

The flaking door panel is tied to the wall next to it with a metal wire. He takes the lighter out of his pocket and flicks it on: the hook is still around the nail, and two chrome hinges shine in the light of the flame. The door scrapes against the ground, blocked by a raised root: he can't open it all the way. He ducks his head to go inside, and is immediately met by a waft of warm air, of things rotting. He lights up the inside: the crooked walls, the worn-out sponge of a bathmat – a small find from the beach. In the half-light, on two stumps he found in the clearing, are the things he stole from that first house hidden by the trees: a family photo, a candle, a plate and two pieces of cutlery. Then, a week later, from the detached house behind Gemma's shop: a mug that says BUONGIORNO, a toothbrush and a screwdriver.

He sits on the spongy bathmat, in the dark, and hugs his legs. His family are asleep; there's just over a mile between them, just a half-hour walk, but really, it's an entire universe.

What are you thinking about? His mother's voice comes to him like the rushing of a summer breeze through the grass. *You're so quiet recently.*

He imagines losing himself in the woods or living by himself in the shack, like a young hermit, only heading down to Cave, Ponte or Rivafredda to find something to eat, blankets, or any tools he might need. Drinking and washing at the stream. He imagines his torn clothing, his battered trainers. Bringing his solitude to completion.

Leaning against a wall, he flicks the lighter on and off. In the dark, he hears a soft crackling: the sound of leaves being stepped on where the ground dips. He flicks the flame back on, aiming it at the door, at the darkness, and he goes still, listening.

Whatever it was, he thinks, it must have gone away.

The second house, that detached home behind Gemma's shop, had a window already open – it was much easier.

As soon as he was inside, he asked: 'Anyone home?'

Rectangles of light on the floors and carpets, and the sound of his own footsteps. The BUONGIORNO mug, still holding the dregs of someone's coffee, sat on the dining table. The screwdriver was on the lid of a large jar of lotion next to the basin in the downstairs bathroom. That was where he filled the bathtub. He let the water start to overflow, then turned off the tap. He pocketed one of the three toothbrushes, headed back to the kitchen with the screwdriver and hid it, along with the mug, inside his hoodie pocket. He found a pen and a small notepad in the lounge: he ripped out a page, wrote on it *Sorry to bother you* and then set it on fire. On their return, the owners would find a bathtub full of water and some scraps of burnt paper.

In the morning sun he reached the gate; he strained his ears – just a dog barking and the echoes of a radio – then climbed over it. In that moment, as he was jumping down, the screwdriver fell from his pocket: he leaned over to pick it up just as a car turned onto the street. Initially, the man driving saw nothing but a figure in dark clothing bending over the pavement. But then he slowed down and drove along next to him, turning round to get a proper look, or maybe he just peered in his wing mirror. But he saw his long hair, his back and arms encased in the hoodie, his black trousers. The flash of his hood, pulled up too late. He recognised him, or so he thought, and talked about it with Gemma and Carlo, at the shop. 'I saw him out on the street, just yesterday morning. He ran away. It was him, if you ask me.'

Neither of them really believe the driver.

He carried the stolen things to his shack and put them down on the logs. He left just in time, a hand pressed to his mouth, and was sick over the dry leaves.

There's a spot in the grassy clearing, to the right of the rusty trailer, from where you can just about see a bend in the river. Molten metal, poured into the valley. In summer, before it became a tip, he would often go to the beach with his family. Back then he was just a little boy who liked to swim. He and his sisters would go as far as the small island, with its tall, thick reeds growing up among the bushes. They'd step out of the water, almost always cold, onto a thin strip of gravel mixed with sand and warm up in the sun, rubbing their freezing arms and legs.

One day he'd asked Angela and Amelia: 'Can I stay here?'

Their mother was watching them from the beach; she'd raised an arm to wave at them. Their father, on a folding chair, was reading a newspaper.

'Mum and Daddy would come to get you.'

'But I like it here.'

'What do you like so much about it?'

'I don't know.'

Hiding in the reeds, he would watch them get dressed again, pick up their chairs, bags and towels, start along the path and disappear, headed for the car. At dusk, the beach was silent and empty. Then darkness would fall; around him, the running of water and the warm whisper of the leaves; the vastness of the woods. The moon the tip of a finger pointed at the world.

No one has found the shack, at least not yet: the door is always shut and his things are always in order.

The previous week, as he was pulling out grass from around the spongy bathmat, a boy and a girl arrived in the clearing. He heard their voices and he slipped out and watched them unobserved, squatting on his heels among the weeds behind the cluster of trees. They lay in the shade of the pine tree, kissing. Then they stood up, and he saw them walk away hand in hand.

On those final days, despite thinking of himself as a hermit, he has considered bringing one of his classmates to the shack: a skinny guy with black eyes and a very strange laugh.

Hiccup Laugh – that's what he calls him in his head – is the only person he's really bonded with in the first months of secondary school, and the only one to invite him round to his house. He helped him with his homework then they played Atari.

Hiccup Laugh often talked about girls, about football, about a new video game: 'Which one's your favourite?' He never knew what to say – it was as if he'd been speaking a foreign language, completely indecipherable. He'd just look at him.

'Why are you staring at me?' Hiccup Laugh would ask.

'I'm not staring.'

'Yes you are.'

'Sorry.'

'And you're always quiet. Even in class. They're right – you're a fucking weirdo.'

The last time he went to Hiccup Laugh's place, he told him: 'I need to use the bathroom.' He opened up the cupboards and took a peek, leaving them open, and shoved a piece of a bar of soap into his pocket – a small souvenir. Hiccup Laugh stopped inviting him over.

He could show him the shack: maybe he'd like it. They could sit on the mat with their legs crossed and the candle slowly burning down, like survivors. He could tell him about the two houses he'd broken into.

So it was you? Cool. And how did you find this place?
I built it.
And you always come here alone?
Well, now you know where it is too.

He rocks back and forth, then suddenly reaches an arm out towards the logs, grabs the screwdriver and slides it out of the darkness, wielding it like a knife.

You need to go now, he thinks. Come on.

He loops the hook back around the nail, feeling the wall. The night is even brighter in the grassy clearing, the air transparent like a shard of glass. And he's alone, hood over his head, screwdriver in the back pocket of his jeans, and the grass is rustling.

There are things that come to him as he heads down into Cave, the route a mix of paved road and paths. His mother's hand, for example, resting on his arm that same evening over dinner, her hazel eyes boring into him: 'Aren't you too hot in that hoodie?'

She went to bed early. His father stayed in the lounge in front of the TV for a while, then he joined her upstairs.

Angela and Amelia went out with some of their old school friends, and came home shortly after midnight. They sat on the porch under his open window: he heard Angela's voice, slack from the wine or the beer, her inebriated giggle; Amelia telling her, 'Be quiet, everyone's sleeping.' They were talking about him.

'But if that's the case, what should we do?'

'It's not the case,' Angela said. 'I mean, can you see him doing that? And for what, to steal some rubbish? Come on.'

'I know, but I can't stop thinking about it. Why was he outside that place?'

'Because that wasn't him.'

'But he says he saw him,' Amelia replied. Words he couldn't make out, and finally: 'Well, I'm trying again tomorrow.'

He heard the key turn as they locked the porch door, their whispering, the small thuds and bare footsteps, the bathroom door closing, and their bedroom doors. He waited for them to fall asleep, and when he was sure they had, he slipped on his shoes and pulled himself up, the plate of the moon in the open window.

He slips out of the woods onto the untended field behind the building site he raided in June – an excavator, spectral in the night, next to a Portaloo. A car's headlights force him to stop on the side of the road: wait, he tells himself, stay still. The lights and the soft sigh of the engine fade into the dark and silence, as if the car had shown up in a dream. Now he can cross. On the other side is a house surrounded by a low fence, a weeping willow in the bare garden and a brick barbecue. Along the fence, a narrow path leads to the garage. There are two metal tanks filled with half-burned garden waste; some rubbish bins.

He pulls the screwdriver out of his pocket and rests for a moment behind the garage, his back against the grainy wall. He stays there a while, watching his hands, confused and almost scared, the tool's slender shape in his trembling fingers.

What are you doing here, all alone?

But isn't he always alone really, as he's always lying? And he's so cold, this summer; it's as though he's constantly exposed to an icy wind. He likes the idea of living in the woods, with nightly forays into town. So he thinks: might as well. Become a shadow, a doubt, a story on everyone's lips.

He tightens his grip on the screwdriver's plastic handle.

Pulling away from the wall, he uses the metal tip to carve his initials into the plaster, just above the ground among the rough, prickly weeds, where no one will see them. Then he sets off again.

During the break, at the end of January, he unrolled all of the toilet paper in one of the school cubicles. He took some more from the next cubicle along, piling it on the dirty floor, and set it on fire. He watched the quick bite of the flames, the paper blazing in the empty toilets.

He went back to class with his lighter in his pocket, walking past groups of students chatting and laughing with each other in the corridor. He sat at his desk. Snowflakes glided softly past the windows. A short while later there were rushed footsteps, the voice of a caretaker and the word *smoke*.

Hiccup Laugh joined the others at the classroom door, craning their necks towards the toilets to see: 'What's going on?'

They gathered all the students from his floor in the school gym. He was in the front row, kneeling on the lino. There was a long speech from the headmaster, which he paid no attention to; he was busy imagining the flames licking the cubicle door, melting the layers of paint, then reaching the ceiling, burning the building to its foundations. He turned around for a second, looking for Hiccup Laugh in the crowd, and he noticed he was staring at him.

'Who do you think it was?' his father asked him that evening, his clear blue eyes resting on his face.

'I don't know.'

'Are you sure? Or do you not want to say?'

'No one saw them, there was no one there.'

'In any case, this is very bad. It'll have to come out sooner or later – it's inevitable.'

'I think so too.'

He looked at his mother and smiled. She shrugged her shoulders and smiled back at him.

His father added: 'I never understood why you didn't register for the *liceo* like your sisters, with your marks. The technical institute is a mess.'

'I'm okay with it.'

And then it was spring, and then summer.

There are nights when he wakes up drenched in a cold sweat from bad dreams in which he is spying or chasing and assaulting someone or breaking something: a constantly dark world.

Sometimes in his dreams there's a hole in the ground and he's falling, belly down, his hands scrabbling at the muddy soil, his nails snapping on sharp rocks and root stumps. He is fully aware that he can't stop; he will fall into the hole.

He switches on the light and paces around the room, rubbing his arms. Then he opens the door and heads downstairs, tiptoeing to avoid waking his family, steps out onto the porch and sits on the concrete step.

He hears the call of a night bird. Headlights illuminate bits of road along the dark hillsides.

He thinks about the small island in the river where he once wanted to stay forever, the reeds among the bushes and the tongue of sand and gravel just at the shoreline where he stepped out of the water. The beach, piled up with stuff that people didn't want any more. And he thinks about the shack, the metal roof under the chestnut tree, the stones he placed on top to keep it steady, the rickety walls. The wire hook around the nail.

The last stretch of woods has nothing wild left about it: Cave with its lampposts throbs through the trees. At the end of the path, the opalescent moon floods a river of grass and he looks at the house. He's known it forever, just like he's known Gemma, Carlo and Silvia, who turned twelve this spring and is all long hair and slender legs and a scowl which is entirely new.

What did you come here for?

He's on the threshold of one of those bad dreams he's been having so often lately.

Everyone is asleep upstairs. They had dinner at his place, a few weeks earlier, after the second robbery. After the meal, Gemma sat next to him on the concrete step and put her arm round his shoulders. 'Are you bored?' she said. 'I thought you might be going out tonight.'

'No, not tonight.'

'So, any news for me?' It was already dark, all the lights were on. His father and Carlo were stretched out on the sun chairs in the garden, chatting; Silvia was on the settee in front of the TV. His mother was doing the washing-up.

Gemma held him tight against her. 'You're almost eighteen years old – you should be going on holiday with your friends or a girl.' After a moment, she added, 'I almost saw you being born – you know that, right? You were gorgeous, with those big blue eyes of yours. And you never cried. I remember it like it was yesterday. The best boy in the whole world.' She paused, lifted her arm off his shoulders and stared at him. 'Did your mother tell you what I heard in the shop?'

'She did. I don't know why they said that; it wasn't me.'

After a moment's silence, she said, 'Exactly.'

'I wouldn't even think about it.'

'Some people should learn to shut up.' The sound of pots and pans; a jingle from the TV. Eventually Gemma said: 'I'll go and help your mother with the washing-up.'

A few minutes later he headed back inside too and sat on the settee, next to Silvia. A band was performing on an open stage, in front of a sea of lighters: the singer, dressed in leather, crossed the screen from one side to the other.

'Do you like them?' he asked her.

Silvia barely nodded. She was wearing green shorts and a white T-shirt bearing the logo of a summer camp just below her right shoulder and the slogan ANDIAMO A DIVERTIRCI! across the chest. Her brown hair was lighter from the sun, and she had a slight tan. Twine bracelets around her wrists.

'Did you make those at summer camp?'

'Make what?' she said, still distracted by the singer.

'The bracelets. I'd like one too.'

'Huh?' He was clearly bothering her.

'If you give me one, I'll show you something. A secret place.'

Silvia didn't reply. That's when he decided what he would do. He touched her hair without her noticing, and felt like someone had opened a door – a light pressure on the back of his head, his back – and he turned around: Gemma was looking at him from the kitchen as she dried a plate.

He moved his hand away and smiled at her.

When he was smaller – Silvia still hadn't been born – Gemma would make him sit on the stool behind the till at the shop. She'd say to her customers, 'This is my helper.' She would've so wanted a child like this, she'd say. Nice and quiet. 'Open your hand,' she'd whisper, and she'd place a coin in his palm.

One day he had stolen two caramel bars from a display, but Gemma, unlike his mother, had laughed it off.

And yet, that evening, Gemma looked at him as if she had seen something in his face that had remained hidden until then, or that she had never wanted to see. As if she had found the shack and was about to go inside.

Gemma smiled back weakly, put down the dry plate and turned towards the darkness in the open window.

The screwdriver's tip digs into his back.

The small patch of darkness separating him from the wall is a black river he must cross, with waves of grass frothing under a gust of wind. The house is on the other shore.

He pulls away from the trees and reaches the wall, the boards of the fence beyond which lies the garden: a wilted rose bush, a lawnmower on the stone terrace, Silvia's bike leaning against the wall.

The lounge window is open, protected only by a light curtain. The shutters are barely lowered.

He knows how much the kitchen door creaks; he knows the location of the phone, of all the switches and of the electricity meter; he knows how the rugs muffle footsteps. He knows the creaking sound of the top step. The corridor and the two bedrooms.

They don't have an alarm system; not even a dog that could wake them up by barking. They used to, once – a yellowish furry mutt who was always wagging its tail. He was the only person that the dog avoided. 'Maybe it's because you're scared,' Gemma's husband used to say. 'Animals can sense these things, you know.' One Sunday when he was thirteen, after a seemingly endless lunch at their place and while the grown-ups were still at the table, he had gone into the garden. The dog had approached him and he'd whipped it with a branch: a loud crack along its spine. He had been certain that no one was watching. But Silvia had surprised him: she had appeared right at that very moment from around the corner of the house, a little girl still with her baby teeth and two high plaits.

'You're mean,' she had said, her chin trembling, her fist tight around the straw-like hair of a Barbie doll.

'I didn't do it on purpose,' he said, and it was partially true.

'You hurt him. You're mean.'

'It was an experiment.'

The dog had run away, ears low, tail between its legs.

'I'm telling Mum and Daddy.'

He had pointed the branch at her. 'I said it was an experiment.'

'Why?' Silvia's eyes had filled with tears.

'I wanted to see how I'd feel. You keep your mouth shut, do you understand?'

Now he's looking at the open window and the light curtain, whistling softly.

He turns around as if he's about to leave, takes a couple of steps towards the woods. Above him is the off-white disc of the moon. Inside him is the picture from the dream: the hole in the ground, the muddy soil, the rocks and the roots. He takes a deep breath, then starts whistling again and heads back. He raises one leg, places a foot on the wall and takes hold of the bars.

Now he climbs over. Here he is.

Now

The entire valley suddenly falls silent: the river in the distance, the woods, the night birds. Whatever little breeze was whispering. He is crouched behind the house.

What has been done cannot be undone.

He remembers the dog yelping, Silvia's teary eyes. That day his anger had blazed in his chest – it happened, some-times, even then; quick sudden bursts – then it had subsided, but she had seen him.

You're mean.

A few months later, the dog had disappeared. His father had taken him along to help find it: a long drive between Ponte and Rivafredda, looking for it everywhere.

'You're quiet today,' he'd said, at the side of the road. 'What's wrong?'

'Nothing.'

'Is it because of the dog? Is that it?'

He'd shrugged.

His father had added: 'I know you're worried about the dog. It won't have gone far, you'll see.'

He reaches the pavement, pushes the curtain aside and peers into the lounge; for a handful of seconds, he can't really see anything. Eventually things emerge from the darkness: the two armchairs and the flowery settee, the table and chairs, the cupboard at the back, the black TV screen. Beyond the lounge are the entrance hall, the stairs going up and the kitchen. The windowsill is cool, like a flat sea rock, and he slips over onto the other side – a dive – and reaches out an arm, brushes against the rough back of the right-hand armchair. He hears Carlo snore, then stop for a second, as if he's suspected something in his sleep.

Footsteps in the living room, up to the door leading into the hall. He takes his shoes off. From the window at the top of the stairs a path of light shines down onto the bottle green carpet. Under the stairs is the meter: he flicks the switch, turning off the electricity. He unplugs the phone.

What is about to happen will start in darkness and silence.

He takes an apple from the fruit bowl and eats it standing in front of the French windows in the kitchen. He watches the sleeping house of the elderly couple next door, beyond the fence and a small patch of empty land. He presses his forehead against the glass. He hears Hiccup Laugh's voice – *Why are you staring at me?* – and the voices of his classmates calling him teacher's pet, weirdo, or slow. Then his mother's voice, when she found him at the river the previous week – *I knew you'd be here* – sitting on the pebbles in the middle of the piles of rubbish, gazing at the small island. The things he tells people every day when they're going out, they're going to the club: 'I'm going out with the others.' He's so reliable, such a nice young man, why would they doubt him? But there are no others.

'I love you,' his mother always tells him.

'You too.'

'Don't be too late.'

'Never.'

His father's clear blue eyes studying him more intently after the second robbery, as if he were trying to join the dots with a pencil; the loo paper set on fire in the school toilets; the way he dresses that summer; the rumours going around town. 'You should cut your hair, it's got far too long. I almost don't recognise you like this.' Amelia and Angela talking about him; Gemma's confused look.

He imagines them looking for him in the dark, all gathered in the grassy clearing under a crackling of stars, crying out: *Where are you?* They shake their heads and head back onto the path. Once again there is silence – the sound he knows best.

He is almost the young hermit of the Cave woods.

He leaves the apple core with his teeth marks on the table. He reappears in the hall, gripping the screwdriver.

The banister is lukewarm. There are sports socks on the carpet. Carlo stops snoring again. He's a good man – he started crying when he realised he would never see the dog again – but he's big: he could throw him to the ground, pin him there.

He has considered this; all is good.

In any case, he'll go to Silvia first, the bedroom to the left with the posters of singers on the walls, the yellow curtain, the jewellery box filled with hair bands and clips, small rings and necklaces, and charms. He will wake her gently, whispering her name to bring her to the surface, tell her to be quiet. Then he'll tell her to get up because her parents are waiting for her. *Something happened, come on.* She will blink, still groggy with sleep. She'll recognise him. He doesn't think she remembers him hitting the dog; she was only seven.

He is on the last flight of stairs now, his steps slower and more careful. He skips the creaky step. He sees the faint glint of the bathroom tiles at the end of the corridor, and the starry sky framed by the open window. Silvia's bedroom. He moves closer to her bed and pulls down his hood. She's lying on one side, facing the wall, uncovered as if someone has pulled away her sheets. She's wearing white pyjamas with short legs and sleeves, patterned with large hearts. The twine bracelets are still around her wrists; she has a small plaster on her right ankle.

He leans over and brushes her shoulder.

'Wake up,' he whispers. 'Hey, wake up. It's me.'

It takes Silvia a couple of seconds to open her eyes. She stretches her legs, rubs her face into the pillow, complaining.

'Wake up,' he says, again.

She turns her head, looks at him for a second, and he sees a jolt of fear run through her. She sits up. 'What are you doing here?' she mumbles. 'Where's Mummy?'

She looks even smaller than usual. Like his sisters, before they left, when he used to go into their rooms at night to watch them sleep.

He gestures to her to be quiet, bringing his index finger to his lips. From the other room comes the deep snoring of her father.

'They're over there, waiting for you,' he whispers, then he smiles, and the tension inside her seems to melt: her shoulders relax and she brushes her hair out of her face. The twine bracelets make no sound. She's awake but really she's still sleeping: she doesn't ask him anything else. She yawns, placing her feet on the floor in the pale moonlight, then scratches her arm, stands up and follows him in silence.

'Come,' he says. He hides the hand wielding the screwdriver.

They leave her room and the posters together, move into the corridor, in front of the other room. He stops, gestures to her to go in, pulls up his hood.

Silvia steps in front of him and he curls his toes in his socks, watching her cross the threshold. The metal roof of the shack flashes through his burning mind. The wisps of reeds rustling in the wind.

No one can stop him now.

Entering the house of people he knows in the middle of the night, carrying a screwdriver, isn't that different from leaving, disappearing forever.

He has never kissed anyone, nor has he done any of the other stuff – the idea of sex, the very idea of exploring another body makes him blanch. He's never had a cigarette or a spliff, not even a beer. Never had a friend, other than Hiccup Laugh. Just a handful of birthday parties at classmates' houses when he was younger, and the ones that his mother organised for his birthday up to the first year of secondary school. The memory of every one of them is awful: the terrible effort he had to make to pretend to feel at ease, the forced smile, the desire to run away.

'You could invite a friend over,' she tells him sometimes, when she sees him go out.

'Maybe some other time.'

He's never been to a club. The most popular one, between Cave and Rivafredda, is *Laguna Blu*, a long, isolated warehouse in the middle of the fields. Its sign depicting pale blue water and two curved palm trees seems, from a distance, to float in mid-air. That summer he wandered around it, a dark shape moving around the edges of the car park, studying the people going in and coming out.

Everything, everyone is all just a bunch of secrets.

Then there are the things he's done. The fire in the school toilets. Stealing from the building site and the two houses, going to the beach. His bad dreams. Screaming with rage, sometimes, when he's alone in the shack. Knocking one out on the ledge of the bath-tub or in the shadow of the garage, when there's no one at home. Doing it in the woods, behind bushes and thorns, watching couples making out; or between the slashes of light filtering through the ramshackle walls of the shack, thinking of Hiccup Laugh or this or that girl he'd seen around Cave. Sticky fingers, all that pant-ing, those grunts he's ashamed of, afterwards. Keep smiling, keep being kind. Lying all the time – he's such a fucking liar.

This is how it really begins: Silvia watching her still-sleep-ing parents and then turning around, seeing his hood up on his head, something glinting in his hand. It must look strange. And there's something else strange: the lights are off. Whatever is left of her sleep vanishes completely.

'Mummy, wake up. Daddy?' She's still whispering, almost as if she's afraid of breaking a pact.

Gemma moves her legs under the sheet: her daughter's voice has reached her, wherever she was. 'What's up?' she says.

The room, far away from the road, looks out onto the woods. Gemma sits up in bed as if a pair of ropes has pulled her up by the shoulders. 'What's going on, my love?'

'Mummy,' Silvia says again, turning to point at him. 'He came to wake me up.'

And then she sees him, a dark shape, and she's startled, she brings a hand to her chest, before she recognises him. 'My God. Oh Lord, you gave me such a fright.'

She asks him what he's doing there, and nudges her husband's arm, shaking him gently.

'He was in my bedroom, Mummy.'

'What? What do you mean?'

'Did you tell him to come and wake me up?'

'No, darling.'

Carlo turns around in the bed, asks in his cavernous voice: 'What's going on?' but Gemma doesn't reply. So the man follows his wife's gaze, raising his head from the pillow, up to his daughter and the hooded figure next to the door. He bolts upright: 'What the fuck.'

Gemma says: 'It's him.' She speaks his name. They both try to switch on the lights.

Silvia asks again: 'Did you tell him to come?' She goes over to her mother, stopping between the bed and the window, in the dark bedroom.

He takes a step forward. 'I shut it off.'

'What?'

'The electricity, the lights – all of it. Sit down,' he tells Silvia, gently. 'You need to stay down. Sit.'

'Is this some sort of joke?' Carlo asks. A brief laugh escapes him, as if there is no other possibility.

'No.'

'Do your parents know you're here?'

He shakes his head.

'Has something happened?' Carlo pulls the sheet aside, swinging his legs towards the edge of the bed. He's wearing pants and a vest. Dark hair on his strong thighs, on his shoulders, on his large forearms.

'Stay still, please,' he says. He raises his hand, shows the screwdriver, a metallic flash in the dark.

'What is that supposed to be?'

Gemma pulls her daughter close to her, holds her in her arms: they're like one being. He can hear her murmur, 'Oh God, I can't believe it. It really was you?'

It wasn't me.

I almost saw you being born, you know that, right?

What we appear to be doesn't really matter, he thinks.

Carlo's feet are on the floor. 'Come on, go home,' he says. As far as he's concerned, this is still just a bad joke; they might even be able to laugh about it in the morning. But then he clears his throat, staring at the door. 'How did you get in?' He thinks he can see Carlo's thoughts travel through him and down the stairs, stop in the hall and head into the lounge – the open shutters, the open window – before quickly coming back to the bedroom.

'I don't want to hurt you,' he says.

Silvia turns to Gemma: 'What is he saying, Mummy?'

'Nothing. He's going home now, don't worry.'

'Listen,' Carlo says. 'This isn't funny. Put that thing back in your pocket.'

'I can't.'

'Put it back and go home.' Now his words are a cold wind. A film of light has slowly filled the room: it lands on his dark hoodie, on the white sheet, on everything they're wearing and on their hair, their naked arms, their strained faces.

'Go home, I said.'

'No.'

Gemma's voice has become a wheeze: 'Wouldn't it be better to turn the lights on? So we can talk about this?'

Carlo turns towards the radio alarm, which is clearly off, and tries pressing a button. 'What time is it?'

'It's still early,' he says.

'What do you mean, early?'

'It means there's time.'

'Time for what?'

'If there's a problem, we can solve it,' Gemma tells him. Despite her knowing – *It really was you* – she can't know what he has in mind, nor how it will end. She doesn't know about the shack. She has never seen him lurking in a car park, or wandering in the woods or along the streets of Cave at night, peering over fences, stealing from a building site. She doesn't know him at all. Millions of thoughts elude her, and still she insists: 'We can sort this out, I know we can.'

'I'm afraid not,' he tells her.

'How does this make any sense? I don't understand – we care about you.'

'About who?'

Gemma stays silent, almost afraid of answering, then she tries: 'About you.' So he turns around, closes the door, locks it, and pockets the key.

Carlo has joined his wife and daughter. Their faces are three white stains. 'Will you please tell me what you want?'

'I want you to be quiet.'

'You need to open the door again. Don't get into trouble.'

'I already am, seems to me.'

'Then don't make it worse.'

He tightens his grip on the screwdriver. Worse than what? His forehead is cold and damp, his mouth parched, his hair drenched in sweat. Weakly, he kicks the side of the bed, asking: 'Is this worse?' Then another kick, stronger, and another and another. A surge of anger, like hitting a dog or starting a fire. Scorched earth, all around.

Something moves in the woods. Dozens of birds – or so it seems to him – rise into the sky in silence.

Silvia screams, so fast and high-pitched that it leaves no trace. Gemma leans over her, and her daughter mutters something into her mother's chest; it looks like she's saying: 'It's not fair.' Louder, she says, 'Make him go away.'

He lowers his hood a little, wiping a hand across his forehead. The bedroom gets darker for a moment, like silty water.

He hears the girl sniff.

'I'm calm now,' he says.

Carlo hasn't moved. He would already have reacted, if he didn't know him. What he doesn't get is that he's wrong: he doesn't know him. He's kind and good and smiling. He's top of the class. He's a little thief, a liar, a weirdo. A peeping Tom, a shadow wandering around a car park. He is all of these things, and together he is nothing at all.

'What's happening to you?' Carlo asks. 'You know you can tell us.'

'It's a big mess. All of it. Me. A fucking mess.' The man shakes his head, says it isn't true, and so he raises his arm: 'Do you or don't you see what I'm holding?'

'I see it, yes.'

'Do you think I'm going to use it?'

'I think you've made some mistakes. I made many at your age, too.'

'You've got nothing to do with this – not you, not anyone else. No one is like me.'

'We all have something to do with it, in some way.'

'Bollocks.'

'Maybe that's why you came here, don't you think? So we could understand.'

'What is there to understand?'

'You tell me.'

'I don't know. And it's all bollocks, I said.'

'You're just a boy.'

The birds, silenced, freeze mid-flight.

He wants to ask him: 'Say it again.' Wants to tell him: 'Again. Please.' He imagines the stones rolling off the metal roof, and the shack opened up, light finally hitting the mat. The nails pulled out of the wood, the walls taken down. The things he stole returned to their owners. His steps on the path retraced, backwards.

Then Gemma speaks, and her voice is filled with contempt: 'You want to steal something, don't you? So do it. Take what you want and leave.'

They're all quiet, suspended in the light that muffled the dark, then Silvia mutters: 'I need a wee.'

'Did you hear her?' Carlo says. 'Let her go to the bathroom. Let both of them go. I'll stay here with you. We can calm down, call your parents, and sort this all out.'

Now he paces back and forth, patting the screwdriver against his side. His parents will still be asleep. He sees them waking up as the phone rings, getting into the car and driving down to Cave, appearing in this bedroom. And he starts to scream, pressing his hands over his ears, as if he were alone inside his shack.

But he's still in the bedroom.

Silvia is whimpering. She has opened her legs a little: she touches the sheet, then her damp pyjama shorts.

When she realises what has happened, Gemma pulls her daughter to her, holds her head there against her shoulder. She murmurs: 'It's not important, don't worry.' Then she turns to him: 'See what you made her do?' Hatred shuts out the fear. 'See?'

Gemma's face is half in the light, and the side of her facing the window is almost shining. The other side throbs purple with rage.

'Open the door, now.' She pronounces every syllable clearly, as if she were the one holding the screwdriver and would have no problem shoving it into his neck.

He moves closer to the headboard. He watches the girl shivering against her mother's chest, and Carlo, who has moved closer to the bedside table, his elbows on his knees, his fingers on his forehead.

The woman yanks at the sheet, at the urine stain, pulling it off the mattress, and bundles it up against her daughter's legs.

'Open it now, I said!' Gemma cries. The fury of a moment ago suddenly dissipates, melting into tears. Carlo moves to touch her shoulder but Gemma pulls away brusquely. 'Don't touch me.'

He moves the screwdriver again, waving it through the warm air in strange patterns – lines and circles – as if he were asking for help through coded messages. Or perhaps as a threat, because he could lose control, and that is why Carlo reaches out his arms, showing him the palms of his hands.

'Put it down. Put it down.'

Gemma and her daughter sob even louder. They have no idea how split in two he feels right now: he's in one of those bad dreams in which he's a person capable of attacking someone, striking blindly, and in another one entirely in which he begs for forgiveness, hands them the screwdriver, lets them go downstairs, and reconnects the phone and the lights.

'Put it down,' Carlo says again. 'Please.'

After

What he did after that was to ask Silvia to follow him.

Gemma and her husband raised their voices: they said no, absolutely not, they wouldn't let her go. Gemma clutched her to her chest as the girl kept sobbing.

'Listen,' said Carlo, but he shook his head, grabbed Silvia by the wrist and when her father kneeled on the bed trying to hold her back, he shouted: 'Don't move!' He pulled until the girl was on her feet, her hair covering her face.

'Don't cry,' he whispered in her ear. 'It's almost over now.'

Gemma wailed as her husband insisted: 'Listen,' hoping to convince him. 'What do you need her for?'

'Nothing.'

He ran his left arm across her shoulders, her body small and swaying, and pushed her towards the door, keeping an eye on her parents – two shadows getting out of the bed – still aiming the screwdriver at them. He took the key out of his pocket, opened the door, then shoved Silvia into the corridor; he stepped out behind her and closed the door just in time. One of her parents yanked the handle down, again and again. They slammed against the wood. Gemma was still wailing and he heard her husband say, 'Calm down.' The pounding stopped and he imagined Carlo must have put his arms around his wife. 'He'll leave now, you'll see,' he heard him say. Then Carlo called out to his daughter and tried to reassure her: 'Don't worry, my love,' adding, unexpectedly, 'You don't need to be afraid of him.'

Silvia was shaking, as if the corridor were shrinking around her. As if she'd been shoved into a bag.

'What do you want to do to me?' she asked.

'Everything's all right,' he said.

He put the screwdriver back in his pocket. 'I've put it away,' he told her, raising his hands as her parents started calling out to her and banging on the door again. 'See? It's gone.'

'Are you going to leave now?' Silvia asked, looking down at her feet.

He took her by the elbow. They went back into her room, where the curtain was wafting in the warm breeze and he pushed the door to, told her to get changed if she wanted, wear something clean. 'I won't look,' he added. 'You're almost a woman.' But she didn't move. 'Okay. As you wish.'

He pulled the top sheet back across the bed and sat on it. The light of the lampposts outside streaked the darkness in the room.

'What do you want to do to me?' Silvia asked again. She had put a finger in her mouth. 'I want to go back to my mummy.'

'Of course.' He rubbed his cold hands against his jeans. He could feel the weight of the hood, as if it were a helmet. 'Do you like summer camp?'

The question threw her off. In the light coming up from the street he saw her nod, almost imperceptibly, without removing the finger from her mouth.

'What do you do all day?'

'We play games,' she said.

'What kind of games?'

'I can't remember. Lots of different ones. Volleyball.'

'What else?'

'Sometimes we go on walks.'

'It must be very nice. Can I see the T-shirt? The one they gave you.'

'Why?'

'Show it to me.'

'Okay.' She opened the wardrobe and disappeared behind the door.

Gemma's voice was a taut string: 'Darling, is everything okay?'

She took out the T-shirt; he reached out for it and she handed it to him. 'Can I keep it?'

Silvia nodded again. He folded it as best he could. 'It must be very nice,' he said again. 'I'm always alone.' He had never been to summer camp, he said, even though his parents would have liked him to go. He wouldn't have made it. 'I'm not good at being with other people. I don't know how.' Then he said that he was cold and he couldn't get warm.

'But are you going to leave now?'

'I think so, yes.'

He looked around him. He stood up with the T-shirt under his arm, rummaged in the jewellery box on the chest of drawers and took out two bracelets and a ring.

'Do you remember the dog?' he asked her.

She was behind him and she didn't reply, or he didn't hear her against the sound of Carlo and Gemma's voices, their banging on the door.

'You said I was mean.' He gripped the bracelets and the ring tighter in his fist. He wanted to tell her that it was a part of him, or that it looked like it was: the *things* he had done. All he said was: 'I don't know why.' Then he told her about the shack, said that he could show it to her. 'You'd like it. We could stay there together – it could be an adventure.'

Silvia started whimpering again.

'Now what?' he asked.

She lifted her head a little: when her eyes met his, under the hood, she immediately looked down again. She cast a desperate sideways glance to the slightly open door, to her parents' voices: 'We're here, darling.'

'You're not listening to me,' he said. He moved closer, took her chin between his thumb and index finger and squeezed. 'I don't want to hurt you. Not you. Look at me.'

Silvia blinked rapidly at the ceiling.

'You don't want to come, do you? To my special place.'

He saw her shake her head.

'I already knew that.'

A damp lock of hair had stuck to her cheek: he peeled it away, placed it back behind her ear. 'Open your hand,' he said. He had to tell her twice. Her palm slowly appeared from between her clenched fingers.

He handed her the key. 'Wait before you open the door. Not right away, do you understand?'

Silvia didn't even lower her arm.

'Goodbye, then,' he said. 'Go and have fun for both of us.'

He left the room; her parents were still pounding on the locked door, repeating her name in panic, the same thing over and over: *We're here.*

It was only as he placed his foot on the second step that he realised something was out of place: his toes throbbed, his bones felt like scattered toothpicks. A jolt vibrated up his calf.

At the bottom of the stairs he sat down and took off his sock: his foot was swollen from kicking the bed.

He hobbled into the lounge, where a little light had begun to filter through the open window behind the curtain. He opened cupboards and drawers, threw their contents onto the floor.

Silvia cried: 'He's still here!' Words coming from a place he had long left behind.

Back in the hall he put on his shoes, reached the door, turned the key and stepped outside. He went round to the back garden, over the rose bush, and climbed over the fence: the ring, bracelets and screwdriver in his pockets, Silvia's T-shirt shoved into his jeans under the sweat-drenched hoodie.

He headed straight for the woods, clumsily, counting each biting jolt. At the edge of the field he spun round: the lights of the house, now all on, burned in the dark.

He dragged himself from tree to tree back to the shack, scraping his hands against the bark. He'd seen no cars on the paved bits of the road, but he'd sped up as much as he could. He'd passed the garage – his initials carved in the wall – and the building site, and the empty land behind it. He took the path into the woods, a whiteish light hovering over the ground.

He reached the clearing, the cluster of trees and the thorny bushes. He let himself slide down into the dip, against the damp soil, then crawled up the slight incline and hobbled over to the door, removed the hook from the nail. On the mat, where he had sometimes fantasised about Hiccup Laugh, he freed his swollen foot.

He considered getting rid of his socks and shoes altogether: he could bury them in a hole, be a barefoot hermit. The boy in the woods, with his quick forays into town.

He put the screwdriver back in the mug, then he laid out Silvia's T-shirt and smoothed it out with his palms. The slogan was illegible in the dark.

'See you soon,' he said.

He kept the ring and the bracelets.

He sat until the shouting and moaning, which he thought had followed him, started to fade.

He did not loop the hook around the nail again.

Hopping at times, his hood bouncing on his head, he reappeared on his street. The gate and the front door were wide open, and there was no sign of his father's car. He climbed up the concrete step, leaving behind his shoe, and stepped inside. His sisters peeked their heads out from the stairs: 'Where were you? Mum and Daddy just ran out.'

He gave them one of his smiles.

Their hair was tangled, their faces still creased with pillow marks. They both narrowed their eyes at him as soon as he got closer: 'What did you do?'

Amelia pulled his hood down. They studied him: the shoeless foot, the hobbling, the dirty trousers and scraped hands.

'Someone called,' Angela said. 'Did you fall or something? What were you doing out of the house?'

They seemed to form a single person wrenched from sleep. He thought he could see them at the river, young girls still, on the tongue of sand and gravel. He saw them dive, then slice through the water towards the beach. At one point they turned their heads around, moving their arms and legs in small circles, and called to him.

You can't stay here.

'I'd like to come through,' he said, and they let him pass.

Then everything else happened: his father's slaps, his desperation and rage as he knelt down on the floor and found the bracelets and the ring under the bed.

'What are you?' he asked him.

'Your son.'

His mother had stayed in the doorway, overwhelmed by the phone call, the short drive, the story of that horrible night which she had been forced to hear. All she said was: 'Stop that!'

Neither of them mentioned the T-shirt. They left his room and his father headed back to Gemma's house.

He sat down, removed his sock, studied his swollen toes and bruised ankle, then hopped to the door, locked it, switched off the light and lay down on the bed. He picked up the Walkman from the bedside table, placed the headphones over his ears and turned the volume up as high as it would go. He curled up on one side, his eyes shut tight, and travelled in darkness as the sun was rising. He spent that morning, and the afternoon, turning and turning that cassette, barely moving his swollen foot on the sheet.

When the batteries ran out – the music ever slower, the sounds more cavernous – he removed his headphones, looped the cable around them and let them fall, along with the Walkman, between his bed and the wall.

'Have a safe trip,' he said.

He only left the room once, when he needed to use the toilet. Amelia appeared in the corridor, in the rose-tinted light of sunset. Then his mother, who tried to keep him out there, telling him: 'You can't be like this.'

'Let me go,' he said, and smiled at her, calmly, on the white tiles.

He spent the night lying on the floor of his room, feeling the house fall asleep, then startle awake again. Sometimes it felt as if it were actually boiling over: his father's voice in the silence suddenly bursting out: 'No!' as if he were still slapping him. A chair brusquely scraped across the floor. His mother's voice: 'Pietro, please listen to me.'

The light of dawn unrolled across the ceiling.

At some point, his mother begged him to open the door, then left him a plate in the corridor. 'You need to eat something,' she said. She sounded defeated.

There was the stubborn drill of the phone and his parents having a row. A car in the driveway, and his grandmother's voice: 'Sara, darling, calm down.' Light flowed over the wardrobe, the tidy desk, the empty walls; then it receded.

That day was just a parenthesis.

Waking from a dream, he reached out towards the dark ceiling, convinced he was in his shack. But he was still in bed, wrapped in his sheet.

The image of the boy of the woods – the young hermit – had become more confused as he had come home, scratched and cold. Finally, he saw it disappear once and for all, peeling itself away from him, and he saw weeds and thorns eating up the shack, the metal roof crashing to the ground. His things buried.

He moved the blanket aside and sat up. He pulled off his hoodie, T-shirt and jeans, his left sock and trainer, his underwear.

'Here I am,' he said, as if talking to someone.

*　　*　　*

His parents and sisters, collapsed back into sleep, didn't hear him unlock the door, reach the landing and go downstairs. He took the car keys. He left the house, naked, and stopped to breathe. He looked at the shiny tarmac of the driveway under the full moon, the bars of the gate, the woods across the road and the concrete cube of the garage.

It's not that hard, he thought.

He hopped across the garden, his skin covered in goose-bumps, the grass cool under his foot. He pulled the shutter up slowly, careful not to wake anyone. The tail lights of his father's car shone in the dark.

He switched the lights on. Jars of screws, jars of nails and dozens of tools. He lowered the shutter again. There was a smell of damp, like that inside the shack, with a sharp undertone of white spirit.

He rubbed his chest and shoulders, his long skinny legs. Pulled back his hair.

On the back wall, inside a box, was a bundle of sheets that his father kept to rip up into cloths. He pulled them out, took two armfuls, hopping backwards and forwards, and placed them all against the shutter, over the concrete step.

He switched off the lights and reached towards the car. He was on the edge of that hole, and there was nothing left to hold on to.

He could hear something flowing in the distance, as if he were moving closer to the beach – beautiful and empty.

He let himself fall against the backrest, thinking of the small island, then started the engine, lowered the windows, took a deep breath.

Always

But then something happened: a sudden creaking, steps next to the car. Someone called his name. His mother's face appeared through the window: 'What are you doing?' She looked more surprised than worried. She coughed, then cleared her throat. 'It's hard to breathe,' she said.

'Go away,' he replied, under the continuous thrum of the engine.

'Get out,' she said, and he shook his head. He could feel the clean air coming in from outside, mixing with the exhaust fumes. The smell of warm grass, of dusty soil. And the smell of his mother's sleep.

'Go away,' he whispered again. 'Please.'

'I wouldn't dream of it.'

She sat next to him. She had moved around the car so quickly it was as though she'd never even been at the window. Then she turned round, placed her hands in her lap and smiled. 'So?'

He couldn't move; he could barely keep his eyes open. The image disappeared, but her voice was still there.

'What's up? Did you zone out?' he could hear her ask him. Strange that she hadn't asked him to turn off the engine.

'I was falling asleep.'

'I'm your mother, I came for you. You need to open your eyes again.'

'I can't.'

Her fingers touched his face: it felt like she was feeling his features, as if she were blindfolded.

'Now mine are closed too,' she told him. 'Now we're the same. See? You're not alone.'

The voice disappeared for a while, too.

At one point he stopped breathing. He had arrived at the beach and the moon was throbbing. The small island was in front of him – a few minutes more and he'd be over there – but then he lurched forward, gasping for a sliver of air.

'You don't need to be afraid,' she said. 'I haven't left.'

'I'm not afraid.' He turned his head towards the car door; the fog filling the garage. Another step and the water would be at his knees, his crotch, his shoulders. 'Did you see what I did?'

'I'm not blind, you know.'

'You didn't want to believe it though. I've always told you so much bullshit.'

'Don't say that.'

'You never *got* it.'

'What do you know?' She was angry now, as if he'd insulted her. She was coughing, but she grabbed his hand. 'Sorry,' she said.

'I can't go back, Mum.'

'That's the stupidest thing I've ever heard.'

'But it's the truth, for once.'

There was nothing to go back to – only that badly put together shack, his deluded dream of a house where he could be himself, whatever that might mean. What had been able to attract him in the world – the unknown rooms he had prowled round, the lives of people that kept flowing, mysterious small fires – had lasted only briefly.

'I'm tired,' he said.

Her hand was scorching hot. 'You're young; everything will be different from now on, I promise.' She stroked his cheek. 'A promise is a promise. Even your dad agrees. He's waiting for you.'

'Really?'

'He's behind you, we all came. And we all love you.'

'I love you too,' he replied. But then he opened his eyes, peered in the mirrors: there was no one else in the garage.

'How did you get in?' he asked her.

His mother laughed. 'Well, that means you're awake.'

'I don't think so.'

She stroked his hair. 'My baby boy,' she said.

He lost her again. In the middle of the current he opened his mouth and took a gulp: the water filled his lungs, and it was harder than he'd thought it would be, but maybe he spat it out again, or maybe his mother had helped him, because he started breathing again.

'Let's go,' she said.

'Where.'

'Out of here.'

He never knew which one of them had turned off the engine, or which part of the garage was letting the clean air in, or where his father and sisters were.

They lifted him up as if he weighed nothing, laid him out in the garden.

His mother sat down next to him. 'We would never have let you do it,' she said.

'I'm still doing it, Mum.'

'Just breathe now. Don't stop breathing, okay?'

He tried to nod. 'Thank you for coming.'

The lukewarm soil took the shape of his naked body: it parted, like water. 'I'll miss you,' he said, softly. 'Now I know.'

As he disappeared through the reeds, he saw the metal roof one last time. A curtain of ivy covered all the walls, as if years had passed since the night he'd laid out Silvia's T-shirt on the blue mat. It even felt like the sun was shining. A metallic rattle and bursts of laughter were coming from somewhere behind the shack. The door was open and he heard someone inside, a subtle voice muttering: *Come on, get up.* He walked into the warm air: there was a girl he didn't recognise, long curly hair and a cherry red top, leaning over a fox with its belly open. When she stood up, he reached out a hand and touched her. She turned round to look at him, holding the screwdriver.

Don't be afraid, it's me.

The girl didn't seem scared, only sad: she was blinking as if she had just been crying, or was about to start. He touched her again. *I'm sorry too*, he told her. *It'll be different for you.* Then he went back to where he had come from.

His mother was pointing at the sky.

'What is it?' he asked her. 'Mum?'

Her face was moving further and further away. 'Isn't it beautiful?'

Before it was too late, he replied that it was, just to make her happy.

But as he said it, this was it: an endless arch over the grass, in the garden where he thought he was, and he felt like the sky was saying that it knew, at least the sky knew what his name was and what was inside him – darkness and light, since his very first moment. The sky had seen him, and it had seen him clearly. It had seen every last tiny detail.

2009 (II)

The kids' shadows moved away along the path: they were walking back down towards Cave. She turned around for a second and watched the sun shining over the grassy clearing. She was still thinking about the shack: they could fix it.

'I want to come back here,' she said.

Then silence fell, and everything felt still.

But the breeze was incessantly lapping against the shore of the rusty trailer, kept quivering the pine tree's branches. The grass grew slowly. Minuscule wings cut through the air. A veil of haze tamed the light; dry leaves vibrated over the metal roof. *Yes. Yes.*

The horizon caught fire: it lingered, hovering, and it was as if the entire world was raising a song worth hearing.